THE CANYON

46,000 words

By Luke Jackson

Chapter 1

Though Reuben had already spent more than a month without seeing another living human being, and had spent the last few days scrambling down the narrow trail that led into the canyon, forced half a dozen times to clear the rocks that blocked his mount's path, his first reaction on spotting the Indian village on the plain below was to retreat upward, walking if necessary till he was free of human company again.

Only when he saw the red-haired white woman standing among the savages did he realize that he'd no choice but to continue onward to the bottom of the canyon and, somehow, pluck her from among her captors and ride with her to safety.

Reuben Lee had ridden out on the trail to get away from home and family, farther and farther away each time. From Baton Rouge to Shreveport, from Shreveport to Abilene, from Abilene to Pueblo, though that was a mistake, and then from Abilene to Santa Fe.

He'd been on the trail from Santa Fe for two weeks without seeing another living person. He was glad of it, yet sad, too, at the same time. The people he'd met on the trail had not been good for him. Good at first perhaps, but not good in the end.

Like Isobel, his girl—no, not his girl anymore, just a girl back home who'd once said she'd marry him. When he returned to her with the money from his first cattle drive, returned just six months after she'd promised to be his forever, he'd learned he was too late; her promise forgotten, she'd married someone else.

He stayed near Santa Fe in the New Mexico Territory for a while, lived with another girl he thought was good for him, and another man he thought was his friend. One morning, he found the man and the woman together in his bed. He shot: both the man and the girl were dead they told him, and he rode on.

The long cold winter yielded at last to the dampness of Spring. Sometimes he rode the entire day through a soft, light rain that obscured his vision and left him alone and isolated in a vast gray landscape. He was constantly wiping at his face and neck trying to wick away the moisture with his kerchief, wondering as he did so why he felt so uncomfortable, why he wasn't happy.

The rain even seemed to affect Champion, the small but powerful Morgan that had been Reuben's mount now for over a year. As the day wore on, Champion, who seldom was fatigued, would move more and more slowly as if he, too, felt there was no point in going on.

A slender torso made Reuben seem taller and younger than he really was. His broad shoulders weren't apparent unless you measured him from behind or tried on his jacket mistaking it for your own. He had a long upper body and stood less than six feet only because he was short legged. Like his four brothers and sisters, Reuben was born a towhead, but unlike them, the outdoor life only served to preserve what heredity had given him, and his hair remained the color of straw.

Reuben's full name was Reuben Lee or Leigh, there was no certainty in the spelling. His parents thought the family had come from England, but he wasn't entirely English. There was something of the Scot in his height, in his ruddy cheeks, his blond hair, and his gray-blue eyes. There'd been a time when Reuben was fifteen or sixteen when he'd wished his eyes were a dark brown and that his skin had a darker, more mature cast to it. But now, at age 27, Reuben was pretty much content with what his genes had made of him. His real unease was with what life had made of others.

His father's farm was supposed to have been subdivided among the three sons, just as his grandfather's land had been split among the uncles years before, in long narrow plots that fronted on the river. But somehow his older sister's husband had wangled a share, Reuben's share, and not one of his family would do a thing about it.

Almost since Reuben had exchanged short britches for long, his brothers had joked about his "savage" friend. Isquah, a full-blooded Coushatta, did not live on the reservation, but with his mother and father on the farm adjoining Reuben's. When Reuben and Isquah were thirteen and fourteen, they were inseparable. If Isquah's mother wanted Isquah to start on the chores, she called for Reuben and vice versa. So what if Isquah was an Indian? For Reuben, a friend was a friend and that was that. It was Isquah who had made the decision to break up the friendship, Isquah who turned his back on Reuben's extended hand.

As for Isobel, gray-eyed Isobel, the girl he loved, an older man, Bill Simms, not much more than a drunk, had told him once, shaking his head and taking a long pull from the bottle Reuben had been kind enough to share with him, "You'll never get rid of the girl you left behind. She has gray eyes, you say. The next girl you meet will have brown eyes with long lashes and, yes, you'll swear that first girl's eyes were brown." Simms had taken five dollars from Reuben's boots while he was sleeping.

("You're lucky he no took the boots, too." said a fellow rider when Reuben complained at breakfast.)

With the coming of the rain, game and firewood were plentiful. But Reuben could start a fire only with the greatest difficulty. Even if he succeeded, by midnight the rain had extinguished the last of the embers. He woke each morning, chilled and forced to start the day with a cold meal.

But he was young. Physical discomfort was soon forgotten. The hurt inside stayed with him.

When he camped, he sought not so much comfort as security and a sleep that would release him from his memories. Food and firewood were less important than the safety of his campsite. Once, only once, in Texas, he had camped near the side of a dry wash on the night of a big rain. Once only once, on a cattle drive through the Oklahoma territory, he woke next to a corpse. So he slept with cover at his back and scattered twigs on the ground before he slept to warn him of intruders. Each evening, he set snares, for small animals and for the larger, two-legged kind. Sleep was welcome but he woke often to look about him.

The moisture brought the insects. While it rained, they burrowed beneath his clothes and under Champion's saddle. When the rain stopped for an all-too-brief interval, they swarmed about horse and rider and nipped painfully wherever there was exposed skin. For a week or two after the rains started, he and Champion found relief only in movement and suffered whenever they were forced to camp.

One morning, as abrupt as the coming of the rains had been, all traces of cloud disappeared from the sky. It was as if the horse and rider had crossed an invisible line on their westward journey. The ground baked beneath the hot sun; the streams turned into dry washes. The water in Reuben's saddlebags was a day old, then two days, then three. Even as he cut his water ration, and Champion made do with an alkaline pool, Reuben would dream of the feel of water on his back and chest and look back nostalgically on those days of constant rain. Had he complained of insects? He would gladly share his bed with them again, and trade his dinner for the taste of fresh water.

The sky itself seemed to be playing games with him. For days on end, there would be the threat of rain, the heaviness in the air that precedes a thunderstorm. But the only signs of moisture were far to the East where, just before twilight, lightning would flicker through the hills and the clouds dip close to the ground.

The character of the land changed. The color of the ground shifted from gray to yellow and even to black in stretches, as if the earth had been licked by a giant Gila monster's tongue. He saw fewer and fewer clumps of trees as sand and shale and clay took the place of more fertile soil. Only foreshortened shrubs and small tufts of grass grew irregularly among the pebbles. A hollow in the ground might mean a taste of alkaline water or might simply be a dry hole. As the line of tree-bearing hills receded ever farther to the north, he took to zigzagging more and more, north to south, south to north, searching for water.

One day, he realized he was near an area the nearby Indians called the "Place of Great Waters" or the "Source of All the Waters." The name depended on whom one spoke with. One legend had it the Indians themselves had originated near there, springing forth with the water from a hole in the ground. But Reuben found no sign of the spring or the river he half expected, not even a dry creek bed.

In fact, he saw fewer and fewer signs of water with each mile he rode westward. Occasionally, he would make out the markings of a snake swishing back and forth in the dust, but few other signs of life were visible. The vegetation was sparse and grew sparser, though lightning-shattered trees lay everywhere on the ground. Water had passed through here once, perhaps the whole valley had been under water, but a long time ago, long before the coming of man.

Once, when Reuben stopped to rest his horse and to stretch his own legs, he stumbled as he passed a fallen log and fell against it. The log, firm and unyielding to the touch, had bark that was hard and abrasive. Leaning against the stump was like sitting back on solid rock, as if the soft flesh of the tree had been converted to jasper. That evening, as the sun went down, the translucent resin in the exposed ends of the log sparkled like cut glass.

Only a few short tufts of grass grew among the petrified logs. All night long, he could hear Champion moving in ever widening circles in search of food. Where was the water? Perhaps, he had been mistaken about the meaning of what the Indians had told him.

He could have been mistaken. He knew a few words of Zuni, of Arapaho, of Comanche, but not many. No point in knowing many when a day's ride would bring a new village whose savage inhabitants couldn't understand a word of the language spoken the day before.

He must have misunderstood. No "Place of All The Waters" existed; none had never been. But he couldn't turn back.

The petrified forest, flat ground mostly, had a few hilly areas. All looked as if they'd been abandoned by some giant with an armload of boulders. Though it meant a long hard climb over crumbling shale, he left Champion at the bottom of one such hillside and scrambled upward. The top of the hill revealed only more of the same to the south and west—a treeless, boulder-strewn valley, long barren stretches covered with fallen logs, loose piles of shale and tumbled boulders cracking in the heat. But to the far northwest, far enough off that he sensed rather than glimpsed it, one callused hand held against his forehead to shield it from the sun, he seemed to see a line of dark green forest beginning where the hills had already risen well above the plain.

Excited by the prospect of finding water, he slid, walked, ran down the hillside. Cursing the effort, he spent a long, but necessary ten minutes removing the loose stones from his boots and checked Champion's hooves for pebbles that might have worked their way under the skin. Then, he swung up into the saddle and headed northwest toward that dark green line.

A long, dry day's ride brought him barely to the edge of the forest which he could see rising above him on a hillside still farther north. Only a single half-filled water bag remained to him then and this he knew must be reserved for Champion.

Rain had fallen there recently; he could see the marks upon the ground and in the leaves of the tall green trees that had fed upon the rain; but the skies were clear and cloudless when he arrived.

He rode upward. Perhaps in the next valley or over the next rise, he would find water. Another man might have wished for company over this lonely stretch, but Reuben preferred to be alone.

The trees grew shorter as the mountainside rose higher. By the time he made his way through birch and oak and aspen to the top, it seemed there was an endless flat sea of branches lightly flecked with white.

Just after sunset, he camped on a rocky plateau. A chill wind forced him to don leggings and then to burrow deep into his bedroll despite the fire he'd built for warmth. Again, another man might have wished for the warmth of another body next to his. But Reuben both wanted and feared to shared his bedroll with another.

Above and behind him, the wind sang through the trees; but in front where the ground fell away and the trees no longer cast shadows, all was silent. He supposed he must be camped above a lake. A series of stubby trees, irregular bluffs, and brambles that caught at the pant legs kept him from exploring in the dark. But in the morning he would know more about the trail. Perhaps it started down the mountain again.

He dined on roast rabbit shot earlier that day. Champion, also well fed and content, stood tethered close by. With plenty of firewood, the fire was good until morning. The very bareness of the soil would keep the fire from spreading.

The sounds of a storm, in progress somewhere further along the mountain, came and went on an irregular breeze. Hopefully, his water bags, still empty, would be filled by morning. If not, he was sure he could find a path down to the lake.

He fell into a deep sleep in which his only dreams were pleasant ones. He played with his friend Isquah and did not fear him. His uncle told him stories while his mother moved slowly about the kitchen preparing the Sunday meal. Perhaps it was only the clean mountain air, the faint scent of pine and juniper, the long exhausting ride through the forest, but he slept the sleep that by rights belongs only to the young and innocent. Perhaps it was his right also.

Chapter 2.

In beauty I walk.
With beauty before me, may I walk.
With beauty behind me, may I walk.
With beauty above me, may I walk.
With beauty below me, may I walk.
With beauty all around me, may I walk.
It is finished in beauty.
It is finished in beauty.
A Navajo prayer

Toward midnight, he woke to find chunks of ice and huge black drops of rain pelting down all about him. He was not under but in the storm clouds and the thunder was like the sound of cannons. A lightning bolt shot past, seemingly inches from his nose, and illuminated the granite crag far across the lake. A second bolt followed almost before he'd heard the thunder of the first. It struck the tallest of the three trees that were perched on top of the nearby bluff and his nostrils filled with the sulfurous smell of burning wood. In the darkness, he could hear the tree trunk splitting and the trunk and branches tumbling down the slope.

After what seemed like only a few minutes, the rain stopped as suddenly as it had begun and the storm moved on further down the mountain. He moved his bedroll closer to the fire, now slowly resurrecting itself from the embers, and soon was fast asleep once more.

In the morning, he realized the lake he'd sensed the night before was an illusion, a chimera of twilight and shadow. He was camped on the rim of a deep canyon, not a narrow gash in the earth, but an immense amphitheater in which giant god-sized creatures might come to watch a play. Beyond the dimensions of the theater that faced him, separated by a long jutting promontory, a second amphitheater opened its wings, and a third, and a fourth filled the view from horizon to horizon. The canyon unfolded in every direction, east, west, north and south. The eye followed, from crag to crag, from promontory to promontory, but the mind was unable to form a pattern, unable to commit even the smallest detail to memory, because there were so many more details still to be seen. Each ledge was its own miniature world, divided and subdivided into ledges and crevices like the contours of a snowflake.

The far north side of the canyon was separated from the southern rim by almost fifteen miles of the twisting towers. Its crest of dark-green fir and aspen rose easily a thousand feet higher than where he now stood. Below the summit layer of pale gray granite, layer after layer of multicolored rock descended toward an unseen river below: Cross-bedded sandstone appeared with a mottled surface of pale-pink; below that was a thousand feet of a brilliantly red sandstone; and below that came layer after layer of dull red, some with brownish or vermilion tones, some with purple.

Around him the treetops moved gently stirred by a silent breeze. A family of blue jays were chasing back and forth between two pines, yet he could not hear the sounds of their chirping. All noise, all sounds of life were swallowed up in the canyon's immensity.

He had to go down into the canyon. Had to. He'd descend those sheer walls by foot if necessary, until he found the far-far below river, the Source of all the Waters.

No easy task to find a navigable trail. He did not want to risk Champion's footing on the crumbling rock near the canyon's rim, so, often, he was forced to retreat into the wood and then to make his way to the canyon's edge again. Twice on these detours through paths lined with lupine and paintbrush, he sent deer crashing through the junipers ahead of him but was unable to get off a shot.

Once or twice, he descended a seeming trail a short way into the canyon by foot, only to have the trail come to an abrupt end where the weather or a rockslide had worn it away. The upward climb to the top of the cliff took twice the time and energy of the brief trip down and his body felt more and more bruised and fatigued.

About mid-morning, he discovered a trail wide enough and flat enough to hold Champion as well as himself. Droppings on the trail confirmed that other horses and men had been this way. This must be the trail to the Source of all the Waters.

But the hard earthen path soon gave way to a steep irregular surface formed mainly of loose scree. Forced to dismount, he walked forward cautiously leading Champion. His eyes swept the ground in front of him, determined not to trip, not to wrench his ankle or his knee on the loose rock. Champion too picked his way down carefully hoof after hoof.

Reuben's riding boots were ill adapted to the steady descent and the soles of his feet soon grew raw and chafed. He switched to moccasins—first plunging his feet into a shallow pool created by the previous night's rain, and stood in the shade drinking from his dwindling supply of water. Above him, the roots of the pinyon and juniper clung to the walls of the canyon. Below the twisted trees had been replaced by scrub, mainly buffaloberry, and the occasional stunted birch.

Coyote had been here and wolves. Perhaps even a bear. Day-old droppings along the trail betrayed their proximity. A hoof print like no hoof he'd ever seen before, with the three splayed toes of a giant lizard, was buried in the rock itself. Comforting indeed was the absence of any sign of human life. He might well be the first human being ever to descend this canyon wall.

He had to hug the wall as he descended, leading Champion close behind him, for in some places, the edge of the trail had broken away. Loose stones were everywhere, along with rocks that had fallen from the cliffs above. Once he had to push aside an almost man-size boulder in order that Champion and he could get by.

In a few spots, the trail was gouged by a water channel, created perhaps the night before. Most of these channels were already dry, but one still held a pool of blue-green water that Champion sucked from greedily.

The descent was an uneven one. Sometimes the trail led upward as if the maker sought for better footing to the east or west, sometimes it was a slow gradual descent through a lengthy series of switchbacks, and sometimes the trail almost hurtled down the mountain, so that he had to lean well back to keep from pitching forward.

Reuben no longer felt confident in his directions, for as the trail descended it bent back upon itself and passed from one fold of the canyon to the next. Several times he looked back on his own trail farther up and to the east along the steep canyon wall, and once in a moment of panic, the trail behind him disappeared completely.

He rested often. Every delay was a renewed opportunity to look out on and admire. Each turn of the trail revealed a new vista, a new immensity, as the true extent of the twistings and turnings of the Canyon made itself felt.

For the most part, only raw cliff and a steep unclimbable slope were to be found on his left, but sometimes-grassy promontories filled a space where the rock had cracked and sheered away. Rock cairns, a litter of bone and ash beneath them, marked where others had passed and built fires for tea or the evening meal.

Always, he was conscious of the silence. He could tell from the trees that the wind blew constantly, but it was a wind without sound, as if all noise, even his own breathing and the faint rustle of the horse's stirrups, had been carried away by the canyon's hollows.

The switchbacks grew longer and shallower as the cliff itself grew steeper. The rock looked gray in shadow but when he looked up toward the sunlight he saw it was marked by bands of light green, tan, and purple, one atop the other.

Champion did not appear disconcerted by the height. When they paused, the small Morgan munched contentedly on the tufts of grass and dried flowers and licked up the small pools of water left by the previous night's storm.

The vegetation changed constantly as they descended. Now, low shrubs on the hillside were filled with birds pecking at the hard blue-green berries. Hawks circled in the canyon winds. One passed him, climbing quickly, a small rabbit in its talons.

Though the sun had been well up in the sky for hours, they had almost always walked in the shadow thrown by the wall of the canyon. As the noon sun crossing over the rim of the canyon edge hit them full force, the temperature rose quickly.

It grew warmer still as they descended, though by rights it should have been growing colder this late in the day. Prickly pear and hedgehog cactus took the place of buffaloberry and stunted pine and Reuben began to think more and more about his own need for water.

About five in the afternoon when Reuben was beginning to despair of reaching the trail's end, he glimpsed the far far below river for the first time, a thin strip of dark greenish-blue flecked with silver that might have been foam. He had reached the last of the layers visible from above, this one a dark yellowish brown, but could see there were still others to be traversed that day, the tall hard slabs of slate-gray rock that lined the inner canyon.

The heat was intense, almost equal to that of the petrified desert. Though desperate with thirst, he still could not tolerate the soapy taste of the stagnant pools of rainwater. His knowledge of the fresh water in the canyon below, an entire river only a few hours away, only added to his frustration.

Continuing downward past a second bend in the trail, he saw the river again, and the long alluvial plain along its near side, rich with green. At the upper end of the valley toward which he was headed was a series of waterfalls and below the waterfalls a dozen or so mud-thatched hogans formed an Indian village.

People! For an instant, Reuben was frozen in position. Then, quickly, he led Champion back up the trail and out of sight. These might be friendly Indians, but he could not be sure until he'd studied them. Could not be sure even then. Better to be safe and alive.

He continued to walk back up the trail, farther up than he would have liked to in the heat. He wanted to find a place he could leave Champion for a day or two while he checked out the village from a distance on foot.

Champion would need plenty to eat and drink while he was gone and maneuvering room to fight off predators. Reuben stopped finally at a widened spot in the trail where a fissure in the rock held a pool of fresh water. Grasses and ferns overhung the pool suggesting it was refilled constantly. Its taste—he could no longer refrain from drinking, scooping hatful after hatful and as quickly drinking the water down—was fresh and sweet. A redbud tree grew nearby. Champion would be safe here until he returned.

Making his way back down the trail on foot, Reuben hugged the wall of the canyon, keeping as far away from the edge of the trail as he could and crouching in an effort to remain invisible and undetected from below. He had not expected to find any one living in the canyon, though now it seemed to him reasonable that people would live there. All he knew with certainty was that this Indian village must mark the "Source of all the Waters."

Supper was berries and beef jerky. He could not risk making a cooking fire that would give his presence away. He'd found a place to camp finally, a meadow just before the final descent to the river from where he felt he could look down upon the village without the risk of being spotted in return.

Most of the next day, he spent watching the activity in the Indian camp. Reuben had a spyglass in his saddlebag, a gift from a seagoing uncle, which he used to watch the Indians from a distance. He seldom used the glass, and on the one or two occasions when he had, he'd been disappointed with the results. Objects toward the perimeter of the glass were blurred and only those at the direct center had any detail.

Slowly, he inched forward to the edge of the meadow, hugging the terrain, until he was close enough to see without being seen. He found a cleft in the rock that allowed him to lie on his back, his body jackknifed and hidden from those below, while he looked out and across the floor of the canyon.

The village was entirely on one side and at one end of the river where a series of bright-green terraced waterfalls blocked further passage upstream. The river, a deep blue-green in color, was wider and deeper than he'd thought at first and would take a boat to cross. Although he could see boats tied up by the shore, none of the Indians appeared to be making use of them.

Most of the Indians' horses were in a coral at the far side of the village toward the waterfalls, but a few smaller horses and ponies were tethered near the river. Here, the Indian children played a sort of game that involved a lot of running and tagging with sticks. Everyone seemed to be having a lot of fun except for the one doing the tagging who bore a far-to-serious expression until, mission accomplished, he could relinquish the coup stick.

A group of Indian women squatted on the riverbank making and mending clay pots. Others, farther from the shore, wove blankets. A large group of women, looking very much like the sewing circle to which Reuben's mother belonged, sat outside one of the hogans working as one to stretch a single large animal hide.

One or two older men sat near the river fishing and passing the time in conversation with the children, but the other braves were nowhere to be seen. They may have been farther down the river tending the animals or tilling the ground, but, more likely, they simply squatted inside one of the larger hogans out of the sun retelling tales of their past exploits.

Just below where Reuben sat, hidden in the cleft in the rock, the squaws came to the river to wash their clothes and to fetch water for drinking and cooking. Several of the women carried their papooses with them in long wooden carriers that fitted closely against their backs.

For the most part, he thought the Indian women fat and ugly, though it could have been their almost shapeless clothing. Their coarse features lacked expression. Their uniformly long dark hair, worn in two thick braids, was greasy and unattractive. One-and two-piece buckskin dresses hung shapelessly from broad shoulders, the fringe hanging over the tops of the leather moccasins that covered their lower legs.

On top of the river bank doing most of the talking and none of the work sat an older women, top heavy with necklaces, who had a certain almost laughable self-importance. The other women seemed to defer to her and when she gestured would move rapidly to complete their tasks.

While he watched, she crooked her finger and ordered two of the younger woman to bring her something from the river. A jug of water had been cooling in the stream, and the older woman drank from it greedily. Reuben touched his own dry lips, wishing he had thought to bring the water bag with him to his hiding place.

The figures of the two younger women, and he judged their age more by the way they held themselves than by any specific details of face or form, were also concealed by their clothing. One in particular held his attention: slender dignified, her every movement was a thing of beauty. He could imagine himself walking alongside her, talking, perhaps even being served water at her hands.

A second maiden crossed in front of the first and turned to look upward. For twenty or thirty seconds—it seemed even longer—she looked straight up at him as if she could see where he was lying in concealment. Had she seen the reflection of the sunlight on his spyglass?

She turned and called something to the other women. The slim dignified woman he had been watching with such admiration turned at the sound and looked up toward him, also. Her hair was reddish blond, not black as the others, and her face was paler and not as red.

"But she's a white woman," Reuben exclaimed involuntarily.

Chapter 3

Reuben spent a restless night. His every instinct told him he should ride out of the canyon as hard and fast as he could, before he was discovered; but if that was a white woman he had seen, if there really were a white woman in the Indian village, enslaved, then he knew his duty was to free her and bring her to safety.

Though it seemed an impossible challenge—contacting the woman without alerting the village, stealing a horse or horses from the corral so they both might ride, slipping unobserved up the long steep trail from the canyon—it did not occur to him to ride away to go for help. Perhaps because he had already experienced so much difficulty in working with other men. Perhaps because he didn't know then how nearly impossible escape would be.

Until an hour or so before sunrise, he slept on the hillside near the foot of the trail above the Havasupai village. But when he woke in the half-light that precedes the dawn, he realized that if he were to remain near his campground, he would be trapped on the ledge during the day, unable to go up or down.

Slowly, oh so slowly, he explored the meadow. One foot after another in the darkness, he walked back along the ledge away from the village until the ledge itself narrowed and there was only a long drop to the alluvial plain below. The way was blocked; the only path that led down to the river was the path that went to the Indian village. He would have to risk detection.

Before descending, he reassured himself of Champion's well being, retracing his steps upward to give the small Morgan a pat, and then moving more quickly back down the path to be sure he would complete his descent before the rising of the sun.

He carried his rifle, cocked and ready in his hands, ready to leap to the right or left and fire as he moved. The closer he got to the Indian village, the slower he traveled, and not merely for fear of stumbling and twisting an ankle or a knee.

He was relieved to find as he descended that the nearest of the hogans was still at some distance from the path. No doubt the villagers had maintained this distance deliberately, not wanting to be too vulnerable to an attack from above.

Angling away from the village, he headed toward the riverbank. Even before he reached the water he could smell the river, sense its presence and hear the rush of its waters, the rush that had shaped and carved the immense canyon around him. His mood changed rapidly as he realized how wide the river was. What appeared to be a narrow ribbon from above was actually a wide impassible stream, unless one had a boat or a very strong horse.

A fish broke the surface of the river near him even as the slap, slap of a beaver tail could be heard moving downstream along the opposite bank. His mouth filled with saliva. How he would love to catch and cook a fish for breakfast.

He was walking along the riverbank away from the village, still thinking of the taste of freshly caught fish, when he heard the sounds of movement from behind him. He whirled, rifle at the ready, but could see nothing through the mist.

The same sounds of someone or something moving stealthily through the underbrush could be heard in front of him, too. For an instant, he thought the red men had surrounded him and his heart pounded in his chest. But it was only a few goats grazing, untethered, along the riverbank. Even as he thought, relieved, they're just goats, he heard a cry from off to the side, a human cry.

The cry was not for him but for an animal. A young Indian girl, no more than ten or eleven stood embracing a calf, the animal's head nestled on her shoulder. She stroked the animal's flank calming it, and did not see as Reuben quickly and quietly moved back into the gloom. Then she and the calf moved off toward the village.

Other women and girls came out from the cluster of wigwams as Reuben moved farther and farther away along the river. Finally, it seemed that all the women had come and gone with the animals they'd fetched and there was no one left along the riverbank.

One moment it was dark, the next, a ray of sun had struck the village so that it came alight like a candle-lit crèche Reuben had seen displayed one Christmas in the City of New Orleans. The light spread rapidly from the village up and down the river, and Reuben found himself on the dead run searching for tree, berm, boulder or anything that would give him shelter.

After a long interval in which he realized that no one was pursuing him, he crept from hiding place to hiding place back toward the village. The few trees, short and stubby, offered him little protection. Other, larger trees—cottonwood and willows, overhung the water but he was afraid to venture close to the river for fear of being seen by an early rising fisherman. His zigzag path took him two paces to the side for every one that brought him forward. Finally, when he'd regained a direct view of the village and was thinking almost continuously of breakfast—for he could smell the cooking fires that were bringing the morning meal to all the villagers, the animals reemerged from the gate where they'd been driven that morning and began to disperse along the river bank.

Reuben stayed as close to the village as he could for as long as he could. But when the Indian men began to emerge from their hogans with long handled hoes for tilling the ground, he had no choice but to move back away from the village and the river and toward the shelter of the canyon wall.

His only cover was the occasional loose boulder that had tumbled from above and the shadows of the stubby trees. The shadows grew shorter and shorter as the morning advanced and soon there was no shelter at all.

The heat increased as the day advanced also. He had not been this warm for a month or more, since August. An August gone to ground near Santa Fe. An August spent with a woman who didn't love him after all. A woman...

Reuben had fallen asleep. One moment, he'd been watching the village, the next he was easy prey for a coyote or a snake, or a watchful Indian. And there were voices near him. Indians.

A man and a woman? Or was it two men? No, it was a single man talking to himself in a spirit voice as he rubbed some kind of medicine into the knees of his animals.

A insect bite or a brush cut on the goat's foreleg had grown infected and swollen into an ugly red bump. The man cut into the infection, releasing the poison, and rubbed some kind of poultice into the cut. A scooped out bowl in a large rock at his feet held a mixture of leaves and herbs. The man mixed water into the bowl and used a second rock to grind the leaves into a thick paste. As Reuben looked on from his hiding place, the man gathered half a handful of loose powder from a pouch at his belt and added it to the mixture. Again the man chanted in the spirit voice. He carefully blew a second type of powder on the cut once, twice and then stood up.

The goat whinnied softly. The man patted the animal's muzzle and leaned forward as if to whisper into the animal's ear in reply. The goat nodded as if it had heard and understood. Satisfied, the man beckoned to a second member of the herd that stepped forward, mesmerized, to take the first animal's place.

An insect nipped painfully at Reuben's leg; a second bite followed the first, but he held back all sounds of protest. A stream of tiny ants soon made their way up and over Reuben's leg. Slowly, suppressing the impulse to cry aloud in pain, he raised his leg and one by one flicked the remaining ants off his calf with his fingers. Slowly, very slowly, he bent the leg out and away from him till he could let it down soundlessly on the ground away from the stream of insects. The ants continued their trek along their original pathway as if there had never been an obstacle.

About one o'clock, guessing from the position of the sun, a woman came out and joined the man. For a moment, Reuben feared they would come toward his hiding place, but instead they walked a short distance away from him toward the river. The woman had brought food to the man. She had brought an earthenware bowl, also, which she had used to scoop water from the river for the man to drink.

I'm hungry, too, Reuben thought. He had jerky in the pouch at his waist, with more jerky and part of a rabbit back at his saddlebags. A pity he couldn't get to them, couldn't make a movement with the man and the woman so close. But it wasn't the hunger that tortured him but the thirst. The heat was intense. Thirst shrunk his cheeks, shriveled his lips, constricted his throat. And only thirty feet away flowed a river filled with gallons of pure cool water. He could taste the tang of the river water in the air. Might as well be a million feet away, Reuben agonized, as the man ate and drank his fill and the woman ate with him.

When the woman had departed, the man resumed his chanting. One by one, he treated each of the animals with the poultice and the chant. In an hour or so, when the last of his tiny herd had been tended, he too headed back toward the village. Reuben waited a few minutes till the man was only a figure in the distance and then followed.

With the end of the afternoon, all the men could be seen gathered at the far side of the village where the horses were tethered. The woman and girls were where they had been the day before, although the pot makers had left the river bank and returned to the village, no doubt to begin the evening meal.

The sun's rays fell more and more at an angle until only the far north wall of the outer canyon was lit. As the canyon fell into shadow, the young girls set out from the village in a repeat of that morning's procedure.

I've wasted the day, Reuben thought. It would be dark shortly and still he had not seen or talked with the white woman he'd seen the day before. He had to do something. If he remained where he was, he would be discovered. If he retreated to the canyon wall, then he would be doomed to spend another wasted night and day no closer to his goal. Making a conscious decision, Reuben headed for the river and prepared to wade upstream toward the village. The river was the only way.

The banks of the river were steeper than he'd anticipated. No doubt in the Spring the waters came closer to the bank, but now the river bed was its own miniature canyon, steep in some places, lined with crushed boulders in others.

He picked his way downhill to where only a narrow band of rock separated the riverbank from the rushing water. Kneeling, one pant leg partially in the stream, he scooped the water up in his hands and brought it to his mouth again and again. The cool water slid down along the creases of his back as he leaned forward and plunged his head below the surface.

The next bend in the river left him standing for a moment in shallow water as the narrow strip between the bluff and the stream disappeared completely. A tree limb whizzed by him only a few yards away. He hadn't realized the water moved so swiftly. If he tried to swim or if he fell while wading, he would be swept downstream. He had no choice: he would have to climb the steep riverbank and risk exposure on land.

Concentrating on the steep climb up the slippery bank, he forgot entirely about the women who would be coming down to fetch water from the stream. He pulled himself over the edge only to find himself almost nose to nose with a young girl, the white woman he had seen the previous day.

An earthenware pot balanced on her head. They were alone or at least he could see no one else in the tree-shaded hollow that shielded them both from other eyes up and down the river. He put his finger to his lips, not wanting to scare her by speaking, and watched while she held the pot out in the stream and let it fill with water. She struggled for a moment with the now heavy pot until, finally, she succeeded in rolling it onto the sand. She looked up then and saw him.

"Who are you?" she gasped.

"Reuben Lee," he said.

"Helen. Helen Winston," she replied nervously.

"Hi."

"Hi." A smile crossed her lips at last.

The girl was very young, fourteen or fifteen, much younger than the woman he thought he remembered from the day before. And her hair was much lighter, a sort of light chestnut. Her nose was small.

All of her features were small, kitten-like. Her eyes were gray, flecked with green, and she had long golden eyelashes. Reuben thought he had never seen anyone so beautiful. "I've come to help you get away," he said.

Above them on the bank, an Indian called out in Havasupai to a moving animal. They both looked upward, afraid, but no one came down. "All right," she said, "I'll go with you. But what about my mother?"

Chapter 4

That night, Reuben crept back up the trail to his horse and led Champion to a new position still further up the canyon wall where the grass lay uncropped, available for grazing. He got buffalo jerky and the remains of a rabbit from his saddlebags, and took the water carriers so that he could fill them in the river below.

He would have liked to cook something for himself as tasty as the food he'd smelled cooking in the village, but again he knew he could not risk a fire. So he ate cold jerky washed down with river water. The uncooked portions of the rabbit he discarded, carefully burying them so as not to attract scavengers. He shared the water with Champion who gulped down almost the entire pot. The midday heat had been intense on the trail where Champion had been tethered, as hot and intense as it had been in the valley.

As true dusk arrived—the portion of the trail where he sat and ate his evening meal had long been in shadow—the air filled with a shrill piping as thousands of bats flapped their leathery wings up and down the length of the plateau swooping and diving in pursuit of newly hatched flies.

Reuben had gone over the plan carefully the previous evening with the young girl, knowing they might not have a chance to meet and go over it a second time before the escape. He still was not sure whether it would be she alone, or she and her mother, or she and her entire family including a younger brother borne in captivity that he would be leading out of the canyon.

Helen Winston and her mother Katherine had been captured by the Comanche. Her father had been killed during the raid. Part of a long train of wagons going from St Louis to Helen wasn't sure where, the first part of the trip had been fun. Several other children had come with the group and they would take turns riding in one another's wagons and would play hide and seek and other games each time the wagon train stopped for the night. Then the leader of the group, an elderly man with a long beard and a full head of salt and pepper hair, had been taken ill. His replacement, a man of mixed-blood, was not well thought of. Helen remembered people saying Raoul didn't know as much as the previous leader and that he thought he knew more than he actually did. Some of the people were for leaving the train and turning back. Others wanted to head North to where they'd heard good farmland was for sale. Her father had chosen to stay with the original wagon train, but after the break up, the train was much smaller than it had been and easy prey for the Comanche. She also remembered hearing her mother say they may have been sold out by the new leader. At any rate, the Comanche had turned them over to a party of Arapaho slavers in trade for horses. All Helen remembered were long, hungry days, some riding, but most walking in the dust of the Arapaho's horses. Then, at a big gathering of the tribes which she only dimly remembered as she'd had some sort of fever, one of the Canyon people, a sub-chief from the sound of it, had taken a fancy to Helen's mom. Possessions had been exchanged. Horses for humans again or, perhaps, this time it had been slaves in return for maize and squash.

"How long have you been here?" Reuben had asked. "Five years." Five years: it seemed an impossibly long time.

"I'm fourteen," she'd said, "I'm going to be married soon, to Circling Owl, the chief's son. Someday, I'll be the wife of a chief."

"You want to stay here?" he'd asked, incredulous.

"Oh, no. I want to go to St Louis. Mom says that because I'm so pretty, all the men in the city will be in love with me."

She was pretty. Golden red curls, long, golden eyelashes, small kitten-like features, a scattering of freckles on her cheeks and the bridge of her nose, and a small but full-lipped mouth. In a moment, as the drunk had prophesied, Reuben had a new standard of beauty, and red gold curls were all he'd ever dreamed of.

"Why St Louis?" he'd asked.

"That's where we're from. My dad, anyway."

Quickly, for Reuben was not sure how long they would be able to talk alone, they'd arranged the meeting for the following night. Helen and her mother were to wait for two hours after the sun had set to be sure everyone in the village was asleep. Helen might even want to get some sleep herself so she'd be rested on the trail. "I'm awfully hard to wake up after I fall asleep," Helen had said.

"Well, your mom can wake you." He'd wondered then if the girl realized how dangerous their escape would be.

Helen would get two horses from the corral, two not three, even if her younger brother came. "He'll have to come," said Helen. "He's too young to stay by himself."

"He's part Indian though," Reuben said reflectively, thinking of their reception when they got back to St Louis or, as he planned, when he brought Helen and her mother back to his home in Louisiana.

"His name is Tony, that's short for Antonio. But I call him Pony. Everyone in the tribe does. I think that's a fun name, don't you?" He had to agree. Helen's smile and her laughter were impossible to resist. Still, he knew problems would arise, if not now, then later.

Could she steal two horses? "I think so," Helen had said, sounding uncertain. He would have to remember she was not much more than a kid herself, though her body and the customs of the Indians said she was already a woman.

After leading the horses away from the village, Helen Winston and her mother would meet him on the plateau where he'd first spied on the town. "You'll need to bring water," he told her, "for everyone. The horses can carry it. If we carry plenty of water we won't have to stop." In case anyone is chasing us, he thought, but of course he hadn't told her that. "I'll bring food too," Helen said, "You know I can cook now. I've met with the Spider Woman."

"You'll make a fine wife," he'd said. She'd looked up at him when he said that, her eyes opened very wide as if for the first time she thought of him as more than her rescuer.

Reuben was still treasuring that look the following day as he lay in the cleft in the rock carefully studying the village below.

The plan might work. The location of the Indians' horses—the Indians kept them at the head of the river underneath the waterfall so that they would not be easily stolen—would work to their advantage since it would take the Indians longer to catch up when the women's disappearance was discovered. The disadvantage would be that Helen and her mother would have to lead the horses through the village to get to the plateau. Could they do it without waking the warriors?

Well, he'd know after dark that night.

But he had a night and a day to get through first. The night passed quickly. He woke once, watched an owl seize a tiny deer mouse in its claws, then slept again. Most of the day was maddening and much of it was a repeat of the day before.

Early in the morning, the young girls came out from the village to fetch the goats for milking. An hour or so later, they led them out to the fields again. He looked for Helen each time, but didn't see her. The smoke of the cooking fires signaled a hot breakfast for the Havasupai, cold jerky and a few fresh-cut greens for him. A rabbit struggled in a snare he'd set the night before but Reuben had no way to cook it and had to let it go.

The fields and graze lands for the Havasupai's sheep and goats extended down river for almost two miles. The maize, already reaching to just below the knee, was planted in long rows with the rich brown soil mounded around each plant. Most of the braves worked between the rows, carefully removing the weeds and breaking up the dry ground. One farmer came up from the river dragging a huge sack. Emptying it on the edge of his field, he revealed a pile of dead fish, which he slipped one at a time into the soil around each plant, chanting and scattering handfuls of dust as he did so.

About noon, when it was hot enough for Reuben to wish he were in the water and not crouched behind a rock in a stony meadow, the farmer took his sack and went back down to the river. He had a boat anchored there and it could be seen for a moment until he disappeared around the bluff hauling it up river toward the village at one end of a long rope.

Reuben saw two more ceremonies that day. One involved the launching of a small boat, though a boat like none Reuben had ever seen. Little more than a hollowed log, it resembled the flat bottom skiffs of his river days. A high priest or Shaman administered the ceremony. The priest wore the mask of a fish and a feathered headdress that had been colored to resemble the scales of a fish. He was obviously asking the God of the fish people to welcome the boat as one of their own.

The second ceremony was more difficult to comprehend. First one group of Indians came forward from the far side of the village. These were repulsed by a second, larger group that swarmed forward from the side nearest Reuben. As far as he could tell, the far group consisted of a party of young braves, while the near group contained almost everyone else in the village, squaws, young unfeathered braves, even old men.

The group of braves returned a second time, bringing with them a gorgeous pinto pony. The animal's coat shone and though small as ponies always are, he looked big and powerful. Again the braves were repulsed.

When they returned a third time, the pony carried a clean white blanket on its back, with red and black tassels at each of the blanket's four corners. At first, it looked as if the braves would be repulsed a third time, but no, a corridor opened in the crowd, wide enough for one brave, elegant in white buckskin to walk along it leading the pony. At the far end of the corridor, their backs to Reuben, were an older brave and a tall squaw. While the old man engaged the brave in intense discussion, the squaw turned her back on the brave in buckskin, revealing her face to Reuben.

Oh, what he wouldn't give for a decent spyglass! Who was the woman? He thought she looked a little like Helen's mother, but he couldn't be sure. A young boy near her could have been her half-breed son, but young boys were everywhere throughout the village and if a special part of the ceremony concerned young boys, it hadn't taken place yet. Of Helen—and Reuben had begun to think about her constantly, and the other young maidens of the Havasupai village, nothing was to be seen.

Eventually, the old man accepted the pony and the blanket from the young brave. The reins were handed from one man to the other, the crowd parted, and the brave in white buckskin walked back along the path the way he'd come. He was carrying something—an arrow perhaps—Reuben couldn't make out what it was—and waved it triumphantly over his head as he approached the group of young braves. They danced around him, shouting, though of course the sound did not reach to where Reuben was lying. The older brave and the squaw disappeared into the largest of the hogans while the pony was led away to be tethered nearby. The young maidens reappeared from wherever they'd been hiding—which one was Helen? What he wouldn't give for just one glimpse of her—and the dancing and the shouting seemed to go on for hours as the two groups intermingled.

When dusk came, and the maidens had made their second trip to retrieve the cows and goats, Reuben stood up from his cramped position, stretched himself and slipped down the path to the river.

For a short time, he lay on the white sand, his head and shoulders extending out over and then into the water while he drank his fill. The bats again put in an appearance. He could hear the rush of the water, the sound of a beaver tail going slap, slap across the way. For an instant, everything was still until a fish leaped out of the water almost under his nose. I should have brought some line, he thought, thinking of the hooks and line still up in his saddlebag, thinking of the taste of the fish, the comfort of a full belly. But if he caught the fish, how would he cook it? On a smokeless fire the Indians wouldn't see?

Now if fish were oysters, say. How long had it been since he'd tasted an oyster or a soft-shelled crab or a crawdad étouffeé? Alas, dried buffalo jerky, berries, and a stolen squash were his supper again that night.

An hour went by after dusk, then two hours. He drifted closer and closer to the village, so that when Helen and her mother emerged on the path, finally, he would be able to follow them up the path and to the meeting place alert to any pursuit.

The women had brought two horses with them, a tall bay and a pony. He couldn't be sure, not in the almost total darkness of the canyon night, but the pony appeared to be the same powerful beast he'd seen that afternoon. As for Pony the brother, he was nowhere to be seen. Perhaps, he lay asleep on the back of one of the horses.

When the two women reached the meadow where he'd told Helen to wait for him, he slipped in closer and spoke to them, careful not to get too close for fear of scaring the young girl.

"Mrs. Winston?"

"Mr. Lee. How kind of you to wait for us." Helen's tone had taken on a certain formality suitable to the occasion, but still it was her voice, young and fresh as he remembered. "Mother couldn't come," she said. "I want you to meet my friend Spring Morning."

Chapter 5

"I've water," said Helen, "And our saddle bags are filled with food. We've got squash and a stew I cooked."

Reuben wasn't listening; he was staring at the second girl.

Spring Morning had a round, moon-like face, almost too large for her body. Where Helen's features were light and delicate, Spring's were thick and coarse, like, yet unlike those of the other Indians of the village.

Though her hair was dark like an Indian's, he would see later that day that her long black braid had golden highlights. In the darkness, though, all he could see was a pale-olive silhouette set against a dark black frame.

Spring Morning's eyes were big and round, her face all black eyes and jutting cheekbones. She had an olive complexion, full red lips and a soft chin, a long slender neck and a full high bosom. Astride her horse, she and Reuben were almost eye to eye, but her foreshortened legs meant she was easily a head shorter than he was. Thick in the waist like most Indian women, only her movements were sure and graceful.

She seemed complacent to be the object of his gaze, amused, and somehow flattered.

"Reuben can you help me?" Helen asked from behind him, "I'm not used to riding."

"Of course," he said, turning away from the Indian girl. He helped Helen up onto the pony and then adjusted and cinched down her saddle. "Who is this person?" he whispered.

"Spring Morning? She's my friend. She wants to go to St Louis, too."

Reuben nodded his head, uncertain, then glanced back toward the village. "Where's your mom?"

"She couldn't leave Pony."

"Mrs. Winston was afraid to leave," Spring Morning, interjected. "I'm afraid too, a little. We must go quickly. Or else Helen and I must go back before we are missed."

"Please let her come." Helen begged.

"I am a good rider, Mr. Lee. And a good friend to Helen and her mother."

How could he explain to them how complicated their relationships would be once they got back to civilization? For Helen, of course, a lifelong place at his side would follow marriage. But what could they do with an Indian girl? Helen's maid perhaps? How could he explain the problem to Helen? She'd lived so much of her life with Indians. All of a sudden, he was having to say more words in two minutes than he'd said in the last two months. Shouldn't they be quieter? What if some light sleeper among the Havasupai heard them and sounded the alarm?

In a moment the problem was solved for him. The Indian girl had slipped away quietly and invisibly into the darkness. "It's just us then," he said to Helen eagerly. And then it struck him, "You don't think she's gone to wake the others?"

"Oh, no. She wants to escape, too."

Escape? Then Spring must be a slave. The Havasupai may have taken her prisoner in a war with her tribe. Still, that was Indian business. Not white.

He studied the horses. The Bay was a beautiful animal, almost a hand taller than his own mount, though he doubted it would have Champion's unique combination of speed and endurance. "We'll take the Bay, too," he said.

"I should hope so," said Spring popping up suddenly.

"Where have you been?" he demanded.

"Checking the path. To see if anyone was following us."

"I've already done that," he snapped. They confronted each other, toe-to-toe like two prizefighters: the Indian girl relaxed and smiling, Reuben, fists clenched, shoulders tense and rigid. I must look ridiculous, he thought.

He turned to inspect the Bay again. "He's a beautiful animal," Reuben said at last, hoping to make peace.

"And what about my pony?" Helen asked.

"I've never seen a more beautiful pony in all the world."

"He's my wedding pony," Helen announced proudly.

Before Reuben could ask the obvious questions, Spring Morning interrupted. "Shouldn't we be going?"

They started up the path in the darkness and soon reached the point where Champion was tethered. "Can we ride now?" Helen asked.

"Sure," said Reuben.

"For a little while," corrected Spring Morning, "We'll have to get off and give the horses a chance to rest later.

"Be sure to let your pony choose the way," she continued. "They have a sixth sense about heights that we don't have." Bossy girl, Reuben thought, but Helen voiced no objection.

Both the girls appeared to be excellent riders, though Helen seemed to have a little trouble with her pony. "Pony's new," she whispered.

"How long you had him?" he whispered back, though he was fairly sure they were now far away enough from the Havasupai village for the sound of their voices not to make any difference.

"Just one day. He's a gift from Circling Owl."

"The chief who was to be her husband." Spring Morning explained as if reading his mind. "The pony is part of the bride price."

In an instant, Reuben recalled the scene in the village the day before. The party of young braves conducting the horse and its blanket to the hogan of the chief. The young brave dressed all in white. Circling Owl had given Helen's Indian stepfather this pony as part of the bride price. Pursuit was certain, then. An Indian might abandon a wife, especially a white one. He would never surrender a horse, the source of his wealth.

"He's my pony now," Helen persisted.

"You don't understand." Reuben began, "If the pony is part of the bride price... He'll expect..." Reuben's voice trailed off. He could not make her understand. Not without hours of explanation. Not when, any moment, the braves might wake and begin the pursuit.

"You're not afraid of Circling Owl, are you?" Helen asked; her confident tone suggested she didn't for an instant doubt the courage of her new champion. "And I'm not going to give Pony back. He was a gift and I love him."

"She'll need the pony to ride," Spring Morning suggested.

True enough, Reuben thought, but still he was deeply disturbed. How could he explain to the young girl how important the pony was?

"Maybe we should walk our horses for awhile, Helen," Spring said, "So your pony can rest a little."

"That's a good idea," Helen said. "It's not much fun when you're always sitting still. Though Pony's not really tired is he?" The young girl gave the pony a hug which poor Reuben could only wish had been given to him. He enjoyed Helen so much. Just watching her in the half darkness was pleasure in itself, so light and graceful were her movements. But her childishness could be annoying. They lost five minutes each time they got on or off their horses, because Helen took so much time skipping about. Below them in the village, the squaws would be getting up to prepare breakfast. Circling Owl and the other warriors would be on the trail the instant they discovered the girls and the pony were gone.

"She's delightful to watch isn't she?" Spring Morning's warm voice came from beside him. The Indian girl spoke English surprisingly well, though there was some trace of an accent.

Reuben, still unwilling to accept the newcomer's presence, swallowed his own angry reply. The Indian girl was right. Helen was beautiful. Though the light from the newly risen moon increased the risk they would be detected, it also made it easier to see and appreciate Helen's lithe form. He kept thinking about what it would be like to hold her in his arms and rain kisses on her sweet neck and forehead.

"May I hold your hand, Miss Winston?" he asked. There, the words were out of his mouth at last.

"Why thank you kindly, Mr. Lee. Would you hold my pony's reins, Spring Morning?

"See mother taught me manners," Helen continued as she put her hand in his. A warm glow went through him. But as easily as Helen's soft hand had joined with his own calloused palm, it slipped loose again. In an instant, she'd moved forward to clutch at Spring and then to take her own pony's reins in hand again.

She doesn't know, Reuben thought, she doesn't begin to suspect I care for her. I've got to keep her with me. I can't let her fall back in the hands of those Indians.

On they trudged up the path for more than an hour in the predawn light, alternating walking with riding. First Helen, then Spring Morning, and last, Reuben bringing up the rear.

About five in the morning, the sun brushed the tips of the peaks above them. All at once the world filled with color: bright vivid orange, pink, deep yellows and reds.

"How beautiful," said Helen. "It's so dark in the canyon sometimes. Dark and gloomy."

The warm glow spread slowly down the canyon walls. Helen's hair turned from brown to gold and Reuben saw that the Spring Morning's hair, too, had golden highlights. Suddenly, Spring's accented speech, her olive skin, her thick dark hair made sense. "You're not an Indian," he said.

"No, not at all," she replied, turning around in the saddle and looking back at him, her white teeth gleaming brightly, "I am Spanish."

Unbidden, the words, "Remember the Alamo," came to his mind.

"Not Mexican," she said, as if reading his thoughts once more, "Spanish. I am Castilian. My father was sent here as an ambassador after the war."

"You speak English well," he said, not knowing what else to say.

"And French," she said, "and Arapaho and even people-speak which is the language of the Canyon people, the Havasupai."

Their path took an upward turn at that instant. He stepped forward to help Helen over a particularly steep section. The feel of her young body felt good against his arm; more important, she gave him a warm friendly smile.

When they were back in single file again, he asked Spring to tell him more about herself, "Who are you?"

"No one," she replied, "Just a slave and the daughter of a Spanish ambassador."

"The ambassador!" He was impressed.

"An ambassador," she corrected, "we had many of them and my father was not, oh, so important. But I lived once in Mexico City, and in New Orleans, and have even seen the Charleston harbor."

"I've been in New Orleans," Reuben said, "Many times."

"Have you," Spring replied coolly, "It is a nice city, a beautiful city. It was once ours you know."

"I thought New Orleans was French."

"That was afterwards. After we fought on your side in the war against England," she said, accusingly.

"I didn't know that." He paused thinking over what she had told him, "You're a lady," he said wonderingly.

"Yes, I am," Spring replied.

They had gone only a few more yards when an upward turn of the path brought them in sight again of the Indian village. Tiny brightly clothed dots were moving among the houses. A cloud of dust could be seen crossing the creek bed just above the village. "They're after us," Reuben said, "And they're not bothering to lead their horses."

"It is better the way we are doing it," the Spanish girl said. "When we reach the top, our horses will be fresh and we will be able to outrace them." If we reach the top, Reuben corrected silently, but he had to admit Spring Morning was right. Fast horses would serve them best on the sprint from the canyon crest.

"We have to walk again. I can't ride?" Helen complained.

"No darling. We'll need the horses when we get to the top."

If we get to the top, Reuben thought, but held his tongue, he did not want to alarm Helen.

"You can ride on my horse, Champion," Reuben said to Helen. But it was a foolish offer and the look on Spring's face said she knew it was foolish.

They halted while Reuben adjusted Champion's saddle and swung Helen up into it. Meanwhile, far below, the Indians continued to advance up the trail. With no sound to herald the Indians' progress, Reuben and the girls could continue to delude themselves the Indians would never catch up. But they're coming, Reuben thought, sure as God made woman beautiful, they're coming after us.

They had gotten on and off their horses several more times when Helen called out, "Spring, can you give me my hat?"

"Your hat?" Reuben questioned, "Do you often wear a hat?"

"Not ordinarily..." Helen began. "In my saddlebag, the right one, that's a dear," she interrupted to answer a question from Spring, "I brought this one to wear in St Louis."

"Do you really need to take the time now to get it?" Reuben asked.

"But it's so pretty and the sun is so bad for my complexion."

You weren't wearing a hat yesterday, Reuben thought, when you went down to do the milking. As a wife, Helen was going to take some pretty careful handling. "Helen..." he began.

"What's the matter, can't you find it?" she called to Spring interrupting him again.

"How did you tie these saddle bags?" Spring called to Helen.

"Oh, I didn't really have time to tie them."

"But I told you, Helen, that we would have a long way to go and that you must..."

Who cares whose fault it was, Reuben thought. We don't have time to discuss it.

The argument ended when an arrow whizzed by no more than an inch from Spring Morning's hand and only a few inches from the pony's head. The pony reacted instantly, leaping forward and disappearing around the bend driving the Bay before it. The saddlebags remained behind in the girl's hand, but only for an instant. As she pulled her hand up and to her mouth in surprise, the bags and the food they held dropped over the side and into the canyon.

Reuben had no time to climb out over the edge to see if a tree had interrupted the bags' fall. "Grab my hand," He said to Spring and urged Champion forward after the disappearing pony. He swung Spring up and to the horse's side until they had rounded the bend out of bowshot.

"My hat," Helen exclaimed, "My pretty hat."

"No more hats," Reuben said.

"I want to ride my pony," Helen said.

"You ride my horse."

"Maybe..." Spring began.

"You ride Champion, too," Reuben said.

They did not have to go far before they encountered the missing horses out of breath and puffing, their forelegs irritated by the loose stones. "We'd better change horses," Spring said.

"We lose time when we do," Reuben argued, though he knew it was a losing argument.

"Yes, your horse, Champion, is wonderful. But he will tire soon with two of us aboard him, this path is so steep. Do you have a gun?"

"I have a rifle," Reuben said, as he divined the young Spanish girl's meaning. "I'll stay here and guard the path, while you two escape." He looked grim and serious.

Instead of the final hug and tears that Reuben expected, Spring laughed. Is she laughing at me, Reuben wondered? What is she laughing about? He had just offered to give his life for theirs.

"Oh Reuben, there's no need for you to stay. We'll just walk forward leading the horses and you'll walk behind us with your rifle keeping your eye on the cliffs below. See how the path curves. Either we'll be out of sight of the Indians or we'll see them before they see us."

"I'm so frightened," Helen said.

"You should be aware of danger, not frightened by it," Spring said sensibly. "Now, you get off the horse and walk Helen, as we all have been walking up to now. You walk carefully and no skipping."

But she hadn't needed to warn the girl. The path grew steeper and they couldn't have ridden the horses if they had wanted to. For Reuben, the upward trek was even more tiring. First, he would pace a few strides forward fighting to keep his boots from slipping backward on the trail, then he must whirl, rifle at the ready, and peer down the canyon side.

"I've got a better idea," Spring said. As usual she had come up soundlessly behind him. Surprised, all his attention focused on the canyon below, he nearly dropped his rifle. "What do you want?" he bellowed. Giving him a slow, half-amused look, Spring said calmly, "I can fire a rifle too. Do you have a second gun?"

"You've got to..." he began searching for words. He wasn't about to admit she had frightened him.

"Got to?" she echoed motioning with her hand for him to continue.

"Never mind. I've a couple of six-shooters. I've only the one rifle." Reuben paused for an instant to think, but continued to walk backward as he did so. A head appeared some 400 feet below, below and across the chasm. With it came two bright eyes, a broad flat nose, the Indian's arm rising to bring his bow to bear. Reuben fired and watched the redskin's body tumble into space.

"You can take the rifle, now," he said to Spring after he finished reloading. She looked, he thought, appropriately respectful. "We'll switch back and forth; we'll make better time that way."

Suddenly, they heard a crack followed by a threatening rumble like a herd of steers stampeded by a gunshot. Across the canyon, a section of the sandstone cliff broke loose and tumbled across the path they had just traversed.

"Is it all over?" Spring asked timorously. She was holding to Reuben's pant leg with one hand and to the horse's reins with the other.

"I don't know," he said, "But the rock can't hurt us over there across the way. It will slow the redskins down though."

He drew his six-gun. It would make a noise even if he wasn't likely to hit anyone with it at this distance. "I'll run up to the next curve, then you follow."

At the next curve, he found Helen sitting on the ground frozen with fright; the two horses and the pony, all three untethered, were waiting patiently.

No point in yelling, he thought. I'll do like her father would do, like my father should have done. He knelt and put his arms around the girl; slowly he drew her upwards until she was standing. He kissed her hair and then gave her a long warm kiss on her slightly parted lips. "You lead the horses to the rim of the canyon," he said. "You wait for us there. Stay back from the edge."

"All right," she said, "but what about...."

"You wait," he said, "You be a brave wife."

Slowly Reuben and Spring made their way to the top of the canyon. Curve by curve they advanced with always the fear of stumbling in the loose gravel and wrenching a knee or an ankle. It was easier going now that he could sprint forward up the slope, and Spring, too, appeared to be having less difficulty. They had seen no more Indians, except at a great distance. Spring seemed to think the one Indian they had seen had sprinted on ahead of the others exhausting himself. The rest of the band would be moving upward the way the three of them had, slowly and patiently.

Despite her promise to go directly to the top, Helen remained near them, seeking the reassurance of their presence, never more than one curve ahead.

The last fifty yards to the Canyon's rim were almost straight up. What had ever made him decide to come down this path in the first place? (Forgotten was the lure of the hidden Source of All the Waters, of the far-far below river at the canyon's heart.) This path was much too steep and dangerous. Or, maybe this wasn't the same path. Too late for second thoughts. This was the trail they had chosen, hard going, exhausting, but it would lead them to the top. The thing to do was to think about what they were going to do once they got there.

Helen and their horses reached the rim of the canyon; now it would be Spring's turn. "No," she said to Reuben, "You go first. Then I'll follow."

"What if they shoot you?" he asked.

"Then you won't have a rifle any longer."

He nodded, marveling at her courage, then whirled and sprinted to the top, throwing himself over the edge. From where he'd hit the ground, he edged sideways until he was just able to look over the rim. Despite his protests, Helen crawled forward next to him and lay against his side. A few feet below on the path, they could see Spring crouching, almost invisible, the rifle pointed back down the path the way they had come. Reuben had his six-shooter out, but what good would it do at this range? A shot rang out from immediately below them. Spring had fired down the trail.

Again, a sharp crack sounded and, immediately after, they could hear the rocks falling and tumbling down the path.

A moment later his rifle was flung up over the edge of the cliff near him to be followed by Spring hitting the earth only inches from where he lay. He gave her a bear hug and in an instant she was squeezing him back, covering him with kisses and saying, "hold me, hold me," over and over.

When they looked up finally, they found Helen lying outstretched at the top of the path, rifle aimed carefully down into the canyon.

"Do you know how to shoot that thing?" Reuben asked.

"No, but I saw how you were doing it."

"Well, first you got to reload," he said, and with Spring joining in began to laugh hysterically.

Chapter 6

When Reuben was four or five, his father had loved to gather all the children into bed of a Sunday morning. There they would cuddle together like puppies while his father or his mother would tell them a story. Sometimes Reuben would be on the outside next to his father, imagining it was he who was telling the story, that he, too, was brave and unafraid of anything. Sometimes, he would be next to his mother and then he would pretend he was a child even smaller and younger than he was. If there were danger in the story, even if it was only a hawk diving on a frightened mouse, he would cling to her and press his face against her side. More often, he was the child in the middle, exposed to pinches from his older brothers and sisters. Or worse, they would tickle him until he grew exhausted from laughter. His sister's scent was with him now, her long hair tickling his nostrils, and he woke sneezing, upright on his horse.

Champion was grazing in the tall clumps of grass that grew in an opening among the trees. The leaves of the tree rubbed against Reuben's cheek leaving behind the scent of his sister's hair. "Spring? Helen? where are we?" Reuben said quietly.

It was perhaps an hour after moonrise, and it took several seconds before he could make out their silhouettes. Spring was asleep in her saddle just as he had been a moment before, but somehow Helen had gotten down or fallen off her horse and was sleeping on the ground, her head and form nestled amid the roots of a tall pine.

They had ridden all that day, plunging immediately into the forest once they reached the canyon's rim, and heading away and to the south west of the canyon. They had stopped only once during the day to rest and relieve themselves and then once again just after dark.

It had rained for a short while then, a short penetrating rain that left them soaked and chilled even though they were hidden beneath the trees. When the rain ended, the clouds remained, so the sky was featureless and he had no idea of the direction in which they were traveling.

They had been forced to walk for almost a mile leading their horses, until Spring, feeling the tree bark with her hand and studying the rocks in the clearings, said she was sure of her bearings. Then they had headed off once more in the direction he hoped led to Flagstaff.

The path they found seemed to prove Spring an accurate guide, for it traveled almost straight as an arrow through the trees. They might hope to escape the Canyon Indians now, unless the Indians also found the path or, worse, were already waiting in front of them.

Not once that day had they heard the sounds of racing horses or the cries that would signal the arrival of their pursuers. The only sound was of their own steeds and the mocking of the birds. The Havasupai might be far behind them, but they might be nearby also, circling through the trees, only waiting for the opportune moment to close in. It was Reuben they would want to kill; the girls and the horses would be taken alive and returned to the village.

He dismounted and shook Spring awake, putting an arm about her waist to keep her from sliding off her horse. "We're not on the path," he told her and explained they had stopped and again lost their way. Still half asleep, Spring Morning did not respond to their emergency as quickly as she had the previous evening. The predawn ascent from the canyon, the long hard day of riding through the forest had taken its toll. But she was still cheerful. "I can't wake her," she said of Helen, "Or when I do wake her, she goes right back to sleep."

"I'll put Helen up on Champion with me," Reuben said. Spring gave him a strange look. "All right," she said.

When the morning sun found them, far too early, Reuben's eyes were partially closed. Champion and the other horses moved at a slow easy walk though a wide meadow, golden with flowers.

His arms were still around Helen as they had been throughout the night. For an instant, the sun touched the sleeping girl's hair so that it outshone the meadow and dazzled his eyes. Her soft face was beautiful in repose, pink cheeks, long golden lashes, her naturally red, moist lips slightly apart so that her white teeth showed. Helen's head had slipped sideways during the night from his shoulder to the crook of his arm, but she lay there as naturally as if his broad arm were a pillow.

She stretched luxuriously, her young breasts pushing forward, her colt-like legs extended so that they protruded over the horse's flank. Balance lost, she almost tipped out and across the horse's back before Reuben caught her, his right hand at her waist, just in time.

Her eyes opened then, deep gray pools, in which Reuben was lost as always. "What's for breakfast?" she said eagerly.

Breakfast? With the Canyon Indians no more than an hour or two behind them? If it had been within his power, he would have built an inn for her then, hired a Chinese cook, put eggs, and biscuits with fresh butter, and bacon on the table. Before he could even begin to think about what he would say to her instead came Spring's answer, "We've no breakfast, Helen darling."

Though Spring's voice sounded warm and refreshed, her face revealed her fatigue. Her large eyes, normally round and penetrating, were partially glazed over. Her jet-black hair hung limp and lifeless. Only her full red mouth still bore the trace of a smile. And as the lines of her face lifted in that smile, for an instant, she seemed to him as fresh and young as Helen.

Helen could not forget her appetite, "Not even milk? I do like a nice warm glass of milk in the morning."

"No goats dear," Spring replied reasonably.

Helen turned to Reuben as if seeking to curry his favor; as always, she seemed completely unconscious of the devastating effect her presence had on him. "When will we get to St Louis?" she asked unexpectedly.

His tongue could not form a response. Why couldn't he say the things that beautiful women expected to hear? That other men's lips formed so easily? Was he only just good enough for whores?

These were bad thoughts to have at the start of a new day. He was tired too, probably. Though there was good reason for his fatigue and for his apprehension of worse to come, still the new day called for an inner strength, a fortitude which despite his strong hands on the reins and the ease with which he continued to hold the young girl up and against him, he was no longer sure he possessed.

Once again Spring Morning answered for him: "Dear, we have a long ways to go before we can even start to St Louis. First we must go to Fort Flagstaff. Is that not right Señor Reuben?"

"Just Flagstaff. Town grew up around the army camp. We'll be able to get a stage there. Get you back to St Louis all right. We might even be able to do something about your mother, Helen. If she wants to come later," he added hastily.

"Still, I'd like breakfast," Helen said petulantly.

"Can we, do we have something?" Spring asked him.

"We would have plenty to eat if you hadn't let go of the bag, Spring Morning," Helen said, forgetting that it was her own carelessness that had lost them their main food supply.

All this time, Reuben had been looking around them for signs of water. Water, he knew, was their main need. He could do without food for a while, probably so could Spring. And there was beef jerky, if nothing else, in his bag for Helen. But water was something they and especially their horses would all need soon.

They were about to reenter the forest when Reuben noticed that on one side of the meadow, the canyon side—if there were still a canyon to be found there after all these miles of riding—was a line of bushes bearing dull green berries. Blueberries he thought. Not ripe yet. But where there were blueberries there was also water.

Quickly, he kneed Champion and turned him in a northerly direction. As if to indicate his own approval, Champion snorted, making a sound like an old woman choking back a sneeze.

Water there was and a narrow creek bed, leading to the west. Spring and Helen made a careful toilet and even Reuben splashed water on his face after making sure the horses had drunk their fill and their water bags were full and bulging.

Helen had found some kind of berry growing on the ground. "I'm not sure those are edible," Reuben said. "Sure they are," Helen replied and ate more of the small red-green berries. "They're tasty," Spring said, "even if they're not quite ripe."

"Then take them with you, ladies. We haven't got time to linger."

Quickly, the women gathered a skirt load of berries. "But where will we put them?" Helen asked. This was a problem. Helen's pony had no saddlebags and the bags on Spring's mount hung by a thread.

"I'll make room," said Reuben and began to repack his own saddlebags.

"Tann Chk," came a sudden challenge from the far edge of the clearing. The angry gutturals sounded strange in Reuben's ear. Circling Owl, it could be no other, and Helen faced each other across the clearing. Helen gasped and ran to Spring who, seemingly unperturbed, continued to edge closer toward her own mount.

Circling Owl held a tomahawk in his left hand and there was no doubt in Reuben's mind he was prepared to use it. But a tomahawk was no match for a gun, not as long as the odds remained one on one.

Reuben glanced quickly to the left and right among the trees. Circling Owl was alone. Apparently, he had ridden on ahead of the other Indians, unsparing to himself or his horse, not willing to let anything or anyone stand between himself and his intended bride. A mistake, Reuben thought, the Indian should have been content to mark the trail. Circling Owl had let his anger lead him into unequal combat.

Reuben had to admit Helen's intended bridegroom was an impressive figure. Taller than the other Canyon Indians, Circling Owl was lean and solid like Reuben himself and no less muscular. No doubt he could throw the tomahawk as hard and as powerfully as any other Indian in his tribe, perhaps as hard and as powerful as the bullet from a gun. But not as fast, Reuben hoped.

The six-gun was in Reuben's hand, the trigger cocked. He fired across Champion's flank. Too late. The Indian had given up the unequal contest and disappeared into the trees.

Helen rushed to Reuben's side, wanting only to be held. He was forced to thrust her aside, his every instinct to the contrary, and keep his eye and his six-gun pointed into the forest. Helen began to cry. Spring put an arm about her and led her back toward their horses.

Slowly, carefully, Reuben finished the job he had begun before the redskin's intrusion. He retied the saddlebag, one-handed, the six-gun in his other hand waving back and forth in the direction Circling Owl had disappeared. He could see nothing in the dim light beneath the leaves. Had he hit the Indian? But he was not going to investigate; nothing would lure him back into the shadow of the trees.

He waited till the two women had mounted together on Spring's Bay before swinging himself up onto Champion. Then the threesome plunged forward again into the forest and the unknown ahead of them.

Chapter 7

Saddlebags filled with water once more, Reuben led them toward drier, flatter ground. The forest yielded to a ridge top and they were able to increase their pace, but so, too, presumably, were the Indians following close behind them. Would they find a settlement before the Indians closed the gap?

"Are they right behind us?" Helen asked.

"I don't think so," Reuben answered; "I think it was just Circling Owl who went on ahead. Now they can be sure they're on our trail, they may make better time. I wish we could throw them off."

"How are you going to do that?" Helen asked. How indeed?

"Would you like to come up and ride with me," Reuben asked avoiding the question, "Give Spring's horse a rest?"

"I'm O.K." Helen said. It was not the answer he wanted to hear.

The day passed slowly. The intermittent drizzle stopped at last, and once or twice they glimpsed blue sky through the clouds. At noon, they dined on beef jerky and a cup of fresh water. If there were Indians close behind them, they were staying well out of sight. They'll attack after dark, Reuben thought. We're going to need luck, incredible luck, a town or something, and soon. He tried to recall what towns there were along the way to Flagstaff. If indeed they were heading for Flagstaff; who could be sure where the trail had taken them during the night? We're still too high up, he thought, glancing at the trees; we'll have to go lower down the slope.

A town would be down lower in the river plain, someplace where there was good fertile land to farm and graze cattle. The ridge they rode along was a good place to make time with the horses and to spot their pursuers, but it offered no hope of sanctuary.

Where and when could they begin to head downward? Escape could lie in the streambed that spiraled west and south before them through a mini-canyon. But it would be one to several hours before Reuben could tell whether this moist, pebbled pathway led them to the meadowland below or ended abruptly in sheer rock, leaving them trapped and at the mercy of the Havasupai.

The stream itself could prove dangerous. Only one or two inches deep now, it would rise abruptly if the rains continued.

"I hear something," said Spring. Reuben jerked upward in the saddle, startled by her voice. This was the first time Spring had spoken to him directly in more than an hour, although she and Helen whispered confidences constantly. Reuben motioned to them to halt. Champion and Spring's big Bay stopped immediately. Only Helen's pony was restless, but Helen rubbed his muzzle and fed him grass from her hand and soon he too was calm and silent. Far off, but surely not more than ten minutes away, they could hear the sound of horses' hooves.

Reuben spurred Champion to a gallop, but even as the others urged their horses forward after him, the canyon narrowed. The horses were forced to walk near, then in, the stream. Finally, they had no choice but to dismount and walk down a long and narrow passage where the rocks curved overhead like a tunnel. Though the edges of the rock-filled passage were now in deep shadow, Reuben could see bright light ahead at its far end.

The horses slowed further as the many loose stones that had fallen from the overhang forced them to move slowly and carefully. Just before the end of the passage, the two cliffs closed together at the top; Reuben could get through only by bending over in the saddle. Then they were standing in the sunlight on a narrow ledge overlooking an immense valley which stretched from east to west as

the far as the eye could travel. Everywhere they looked were fields
of wildflowers, white and gold. Though the valley floor was broken
up by berms and ridges and several stands of trees that hugged the
banks of a narrow creek, between, everywhere they looked, were
flowers and more flowers. Toward the far western end, Reuben
thought he could see the long regular rows of green that indicated a
planted crop; he even thought he could see smoke from a chimney.

"There are farms there," Spring said over his shoulder. Her
breath felt fresh and warm as the afternoon sun itself.

"We're going to St Louis. We're going to St Louis," Helen
chanted over and over.

"Yes dear," Spring said.

The creek bed ended here in a wide damp patch before it fell in a
cascade over the cliff's edge. On their left, the ledge rose slightly,
after which it, too, narrowed and ended in a dead end against the
cliff. On their right, the ledge curved around the hillside toward an
invisible destination. "I'll go see," Spring said following his gaze.
She dismounted and walked slowly down the path.

Reuben slipped the rifle from the saddle and turned back toward
the passageway from which they had just emerged. "What's
wrong?" Helen asked even as they both could hear the sound of hoof
beats from behind them.

By the time Spring returned, Reuben was lying just inside the
passageway, his eyes shaded from the sun, rifle outstretched and
focused on the small circle of light that marked the passage's far
end.

"I'm afraid," he could hear Helen say from behind and above
him and then, after some quiet words of comfort to her young friend,
he heard Spring talking to him. "I think the trail goes all the way to
the meadow. I can't be sure, but I followed it down past two bends

and I still couldn't see where it ends. I think it gets wider, also. We may be able to ride the horses."

"Good work," Reuben said. "We'll go down when it gets dark. I'll go that is. You two go ahead now leading the horses."

"But what will you ..?" Spring began. She didn't have to finish the question. The echoes of his rifle shot were already reverberating through the passageway.

He had hit someone this time, he was sure of it. He could hear them scrambling backwards in the passage, scrambling to get away. The Indians wouldn't try the passage again, not for a while. First, they would attempt to scale the cliffs above him. They might succeed, but even if they did, the overhang would protect Reuben from exposure. The risk would come when he started down the trail. If he waited too long, the Indians might find another way to the trail and start up after him.

The women had already left. But not before Helen had given him a quiet hug, pressing her small bosom against his side and kissing his cheek. He thought he might even have seen a tear. Spring, too, coming to fetch Helen, had hugged his waist briefly before the women started off down the trail taking Champion and the other horses with them.

The silence persisted, though the normal sounds of the afternoon could be heard, the wind's caress, the buzz of insects. Once an arrow fell on the ledge near him, spent and useless. But as Reuben did not move in response, the Indians had no way of telling whether he was still there, prepared to shoot anyone who walked through the passage, or had left with the others. Just before sunset, he heard several shots reverberating from the cliffs above him. Someone was firing at the girls, though by this time, they must be a long way down the cliff, out of range.

With the coming of dusk, he felt still less secure. Sooner or later, the Indians would have to venture out into the open in search of him he reasoned, sooner or later.

He was surprised, though, when the movement came no more than a few minutes afterwards. This time, the redskin was much closer to him than the previous attacker had been; the Havasupai brave must have crawled unobserved from rock to rock for more than an hour. What kind of super human could crawl over jagged rock, naked flesh pressed close to the ground? In the end, it was neither sound nor sight that gave the man away, but some deeper sixth sense that was Reuben's own. Reuben aimed and fired in a single reflex motion. He must have hit the redskin, though the Indian, like all the others of his kind, gave no acknowledgement that he had been wounded.

A sudden tug on his leg yanked him from his reverie. Less stoic than the savage and already bothered by a full bladder, Reuben nearly voided in his pants. But the touch was a familiar one. He slid out quickly from the passage to find Spring beside him in the darkness, her mouth to his ear.

Incredibly, the brave girl, having already gone once down the mountain and once up, was prepared to lead him down again. "You'd never find your way down without me in the darkness. There are one or two really bad spots." Later, when they had already progressed some hundreds of yards quietly in the darkness, her hand light on his arm, she said, "You don't need to rush. We've got almost four hours before the moon comes out."

"Thank you for coming. Thanks," is what he said to her, over and over.

By the time they reached the valley floor and found Helen and Champion both overjoyed to see them, he was sure he had glimpsed one or two human shapes on the path behind them. The figures had been several miles off to be sure. Just brief silhouettes against the rocks as, accidentally, their path and that of the Indians curved simultaneously in a facing direction.

"The horses and Pony have been fed and I've eaten too," said Helen. "Spring shot a rabbit. She made rabbit stew. Or I did. After she was gone."

Reuben marveled at the presence of mind that had led Spring to build a fire, secure in the knowledge he was continuing to hold the pass behind them. The hot food would be wonderful after the days of eating berries and beef jerky while on the run.

He hugged her again briefly as he had at the top of the mountain and then gave Helen a long and lingering kiss. Helen looked up at him surprised. She giggled. "You're hungry," she said, "I've got just the thing." She threw back her shoulders so that he could not help but notice her small breasts. "Rabbit stew," she said and held out a plate from behind her. She laughed again when she saw the expression on his face. Both girls did.

"He is such a precious," Spring said, laughing along with Helen. Both girls giggled while Reuben's face turned bright red in the firelight.

He ate quickly. He had no time to eat really, not if they were to stay ahead of the Indians, but their horses were fed and rested and he was very hungry. The hot, half-cooked stew—Helen had failed to stir it regularly—burnt his mouth. But it was delicious and he washed it down with draught after draught of fresh water from the stream nearby.

A fish in the nearby stream disturbed the water as it rose to take a skating insect. Tomorrow when we're safe, we'll have fish, he thought.

They had mounted the horses and been on the trail for more than thirty minutes before the first of the Havasupai touched the ground of the valley behind them. They did not stop to rest. Led by Circling Owl, still anxious to retrieve his bride, the Indians, more than a dozen in number, whipped their horses and set off at a gallop after the escapees.

For a while, the party of three had no idea of the closeness of their pursuers. Not till the moon was up and a cloud of dust was visible close behind them where the Indians crossed one of the rare ridges in the valley.

By this time, the trio had already passed by the first long cultivated field, had glimpsed the smoke in the distance and knew they were near a town. As if conscious of the town's proximity, the horses themselves began to move faster.

For another ten minutes, the mad dash continued across the valley, the Indians' horses in fierce pursuit, Champion, the Bay, and Helen's Pony sprinting flat out just ahead of them.

The Indians were too late. The three escapees passed a farm, then another and another. Now the houses were set close together along the trail, with long fields stretched in back of each of them.

They could see a clump of weathered gray buildings and a road sign, touched by moonlight: "Sojurn."

"We're here," Spring Morning said quietly.

"We're here!" Helen exclaimed, her voice a piping treble.

"Time to sleep," Reuben thought and stepping proudly from his horse, he slipped and fell against the burly hostler who had come to help him with the reins.

Chapter 8

"You've had some sleep," a woman's voice said, emphasizing the word "some." But as Reuben's eyes slowly opened, it was a man he found staring down at him, a man with hard, weathered features, a face chiseled loose from a canyon wall. The face's lips moved: "I'm Mike Forester," the man said. "I'm Ruben Lee," and Reuben shook the hand that was offered to him.

"I understand you were trailed here by a number of Indians." Mike asked in a deep voice. "Apache?"

"Havasupai, I think. They're farmers."

"Let him eat breakfast first," the woman interrupted. Her voice was shrill and marked by a lisp at the end of certain words. "Can't you see he's hungry, and tired too I imagine."

"He can sleep again later," Mike said. "There are some questions we've got to ask him. But I don't see why he can't eat while we talk." He helped Reuben, who felt weak as a kitten, to stand and pull on a pair of borrowed moccasins. "You might as well wear the robe you slept in. You don't look strong enough to fasten your buttons.

"You eat now," Mike said as they sat down at the laden table, "I guess I can wait five or ten minutes to have my questions answered. Them vittles look good enough I'd like to eat them myself, though I had my own breakfast just an hour ago." Raising his voice, Mike added, "Mrs. Stewart here's just about the best cook in the valley."

A smiling red-faced woman bobbed into Reuben's view for an instant. "We had a son just about your age."

"Thank you mamm," replied Reuben, though it was a struggle for him to stop eating even for an instant. The food was good and it had been a long time since he'd eaten anything.

"You slept a day and a half nearly," Mike said and gave a whistle.

"I was tired." Reuben was; every bone ached; every muscle was sore. "How's Helen?"

"Your daughter? She's fine. She and your squaw are staying with Mrs. Flemming; they were able to walk a little farther than you were."

"Your wife and daughter are both O.K.," the stout red-faced woman put in from somewhere off to Reuben's left.

"My daughter!" Reuben exclaimed. How old did they think he was anyway?

"She's such a pretty young thing," Mrs. Stewart chattered on, "your wife must have been a beautiful woman."

"Life's hard out West," Mike said, "there's a lot of us don't have the husbands and wives we started out with."

"The Lord giveth and the Lord taketh away."

My wife? my daughter? These people don't understand, Reuben thought

"How many of them chasing you?" Mike asked.

"I counted eight or nine Indians but it could be the whole village," Reuben replied.

"Havasupai, you said. I don't know them."

"They're from the Canyon. The area the Zuni call the Place of All the Waters."

"The Big Canyon? No. That can't be. Them's peaceful Indians."

"They're good Indians," Mrs. Stewart added.

"Unless you take one of their horses," Reuben said.

"Now what did a nice boy like you do that for? Stealing a horse." She clucked indignantly. "I suppose you had a good reason."

Mike pushed his chair back from the table, leaned forward and stuck his hands out on his knees. He opened his mouth but closed it without speaking. Whatever he thought of horse thieves he was going to hear Reuben's story before he made a judgment.

"Had to take it, to get the girl out," Reuben began. Then, while Mrs. Stewart's mouth dropped farther and farther open in amazement, Reuben told them the whole story.

"So the girls were slaves," Mike said when Reuben was through. While his voice was calm, his craggy features expressed his indignation. "They didn't harm them?" Mrs. Stewart interjected, clapping her hand to her mouth in anticipation of some horrific revelation. "I don't think so," Reuben replied, clearly disappointing the good-spirited woman, "I think Helen and Spring Morning were treated pretty much like the other young girls in the village."

"But living with Indians ...." Mrs. Stewart persisted, as if determined to find something that was wrong.

"Why do they keep calling her my daughter?" Reuben asked. He'd stopped Mike just as he made final adjustments to his saddle, preparing to ride away. Though outwardly calm, the older man was disturbed by what he'd learned from Reuben about the reasons for the Indians' continued presence in the area. Choosing his words carefully, Mike said, "They might stay, they might leave, they might come to parley. We'll just all carry our weapons for a while. I've sent riders to warn the outlying farms. Some of the men will have to miss the barn dance tonight and do sentry duty. Let's hope you're a good enough dancer to make up for their absence.

Reuben's face showed he was not that good a dancer.

"Just funning. Nobody'll miss a few men at the dance and everybody'll be glad to see your Helen, specially now we know she's not married to you either."

"Now wait a minute..." Reuben began.

"Fair is fair," said Mike. But when he saw Reuben's stricken look, he added, "I've got a feeling Helen will remember who rescued her from the canyon, and carried her along a trail most people think is too steep and dangerous to go alone.

"'Sides, I think you're going to find you're pretty much a hero to all the women hereabouts."

"Just the one'll do," said Reuben.

"I catch your meaning. I'm that way myself. See you at the dance this evening."

"See you."

"Why do they keep calling Helen my daughter?" Reuben asked Spring later when they were reunited. "I'm only thirty-two," he said, "Thirty-two's not old."

"No, it isn't. But Helen is only fifteen."

"Fifteen's old," he said, "Why, back home many a girl was married by the time she was fifteen. Heck, Helen would have been married now to that Injun boy if I hadn't ridden her away."

"I have twenty-six years," Spring Morning said.

"That's old," he replied, with unintended cruelty. As if recognizing his lapse, Reuben added, "I mean, old never to have been married. Have you ever been married Spring?"

"Yes," she said, "twice. The first time, my name was not Spring Morning but Maria. Maria Isabella. I was not much older than Helen, then. I was on my way to see my husband, returning from a trip with my father, when the Havasupai captured me. The second time, my husband was an Indian; he was much older; I had no choice. Then, when my second husband died in an accident, the Havasupai thought I was bad luck and left me alone."

Reuben nodded as if he'd heard and understood her pain. "So, you was the same age as Helen the first time you got married." He paused, "See, I told you she's not too young."

"You'll enjoy the dance tonight," Mike said, when he came to pick them up at the Stewarts that evening.

(The girls had ridden into town to see Reuben and had stayed in the Stewarts' front parlor talking with Mrs. Stewart until Reuben woke the second time.

"She seems to think we were part of some orgy or something," Helen said later when they were alone. "She has some pretty strange ideas about Indians," Spring explained. "We all do," Reuben replied.)

Mike looked directly at Helen when he spoke, but Reuben could tell he was talking to all of them.

"What's a 'barn dance' like?" Helen asked. "Will I have partners? What kind of dances do they do?" She finished still frantic by asking, "How will I ever learn to do the dances?"

Mike laughed, they all did, at Helen's childlike enthusiasm. Reuben and Spring Morning could afford to be gay and relieved now that they'd escaped and returned to civilization. Though for an instant of self-doubt, Reuben worried how he, too, would learn the dances, and how he would ensure that Helen danced only with him.

"Give me a chance young lady and I'll answer all your questions," said Mike in his booming voice. "First, this pretty woman with me is Mrs. Mike Forester and she is responsible for all the decorations."

"Howdy, I'm MaryBelle Forester." Mike's wife was almost as tall as her husband and her features, too, seemed carved from that same piece of rock.

"I'm Reuben Lee and this is Spring Morning and this,"—here Reuben sprang to his feet in time to make the final introduction, "is Helen Winston."

"Mz. Winston, Morning Spring, I'm so happy you could come to our dance. I don't believe we've ever had two girls as pretty as you."

Quite a compliment, Reuben thought, though he couldn't see how anyone would think of Spring Morning as a young girl. Still, with her face all aglow in the multitude of lanterns that were hanging in the barn, Spring looked very young indeed.

Party dresses had been procured for both the women, though both protested they'd brought clothes with them. "I had such a pretty bonnet," Helen said.

Helen was given a new, equally ornamented bonnet—which only hid her wonderful gold hair, Reuben thought—of fine cotton trimmed with a bow of colored ribbon; a sprig of dried flowers was its crown. Helen's bodice had a rounded collar; the blouse was higher and more conservative than those of the other women, but its demure collar, and the tight, pinched-in waist only enhanced Helen's natural beauty.

"Am I pretty Reuben?" she asked, curtsying and spreading the folds of her dress, at the base of which two tiny pink dress slippers put in an appearance. "Yes," he said, completely overcome, as was more than one man, married or single who looked at Helen that evening.

Spring, along with many of the older married woman, had chosen or, in Spring's case, been given a plain cotton skirt with a loose bodice that concealed her bust and waistline. The only color was provided by a flowered brooch at her throat and by her dark hair—now braided smoothly over the ears and rolled into a bun at the back of her neck.

Later, Spring confided to Reuben that she'd a much prettier dress put away in her saddlebag. "It has a lace mantilla which I wear over my shoulders while I wait to dance. The dress is green, a very pale green which my father says is the perfect color for me, and it has, oh, such a long skirt with ruffle after ruffle falling from above my knees to the tips of my dancing shoes, like the layers of the canyon wall."

"But not so big," he teased.

"No, not so big," she agreed, her eyes sparkling.

"Why didn't you wear your dress?" Reuben asked, lowering his voice to communicate that this time he was being sincere, "Your dress sounds very attractive. You are very attractive too, sometimes Spring."

"Thank you," she said and blushed, though he could not understand why: it was quite true she was very pretty; her eyes, as always, were large and glowing and seemingly in love with everything around her; in all of Louisiana, he doubted if he'd ever seen a more beautiful woman; next to Spring, Isobel would have looked pale and withered.

"The dress was the wrong style," Spring replied, "You know. Too Spanish, too different from what they are used to here. I wanted more to fit in, to be... in case we stay here, you know."

"We do two dances here in the main, Miss Helen;" said Mike, "the schottische, which I'm sure you know, and the Boston two-step. The latter was only introduced here recently by one of the officers from the fort at Flagstaff."

"Do they do the two-step in St Louis?" Helen wondered aloud.

"I'm sure they do, Miss," said a brash, dark-haired young man who'd been standing by throughout this introduction, his eyes riveted on Helen's long golden eyelashes and her small kitten-like features. "I've only just learned it myself, but perhaps you'd take pity on a beginner?"

"Well," said Helen turning to Reuben, "If it's all right with Mr. Leigh. Might I ..."

"Her first dance is promised to me," Reuben said, carefully avoiding a commitment as to yea or nea on Helen's subsequent partners.

The schottische proved to be a form of Virginia Reel in which Reuben was well versed. For the duration of the tune, he and Helen promenaded up and down the line, performed dosey-do's with their opposites and swung mightily between hands-four. Helen had never seemed so happy and his only regret was those intervals in the dance when Helen took hands with her opposite and for a moment drifted away.

The two-step defeated him utterly and he had to watch while first Frank, the dark haired young man who worked as apprentice to the town smith, and then Tom, a slightly older farmer with one thumb missing where he'd been too handy with an axe, skipped away with Helen as their partner.

The slickers of Boston might never have owned to the two-step done Arizona style. The huge leather boots worn by virtually every male in Sojurn gave an entirely new character to the dance. Rather than lift their feet, the heavy boot compelled the men to shuffle or slide the foot forward, though some of the younger dancers, like Frank and Helen, made it look as if they were actually gliding an inch or two above the ground.

68

If Frank's a beginner, thought Reuben, then I'm a Yankee. Murder was in his heart as he watched Frank turn Helen in, out, spin her around, do a double turn himself and finish with locked elbows, eye to eye with the love of Reuben's life.

Stung to the quick and embarrassed by his one effort at the two-step taken in the company of a slightly older partner, Reuben tried to leave the dance floor. His partner, a Mrs. Flemming, the girls' host and his, too, now he was well enough to leave the Stewarts, wouldn't let go. In three short minutes, while his eyes glazed over, she told him she was a widow, the owner of a prosperous well-tended farm, and the best cook in the valley—taste some of her cherry dumplings. Exhausted, he looked to see how Spring was faring.

Although no one had actually opposed Spring's entrance to the dance floor, no one had encouraged her to join in either. She was forced to spend most of the evening by the walls of the barn or in the back helping the older women to replenish the table loads of food. Reuben could hear her saying from time to time, "No, Spanish," and could feel her eyes upon him whenever he danced the schottische. All that evening, Spring's eyes followed either Helen or himself as they glided and whirled about the floor.

But Reuben had little time to think about Spring Morning. More and more he was concerned by Helen's absence or, rather, by her presence on the dance floor in the arms of other partners. Frank was a frequent partner, as was Tom, but virtually every man in the village seemed to have some pretext for taking Helen in his arms, however briefly.

It was a sullen, angry Reuben who sat next to Spring in the back of the buckboard as they made their way to the Flemming ranch to spend the night. His anger and his silence did nothing to advance his cause with Helen. Though the young woman's body rested between the Foresters in the front of the buckboard, her spirit still soared and dipped and did the dosey doe on the barn floor. "Wasn't that just the finest dance ever?" she kept saying over and over to the Foresters' delight. "And you were the belle of the ball, dear," MaryBelle Forester replied. Few would have believed this barn dance in the town of Sojurn in the Arizona Territory in May of 1841 was the first social event that Helen Winston, former captive of the Havasupai Indians, had ever attended with or without her family.

Chapter 9

Mrs. Flemming talked constantly as she served their porridge and eggs. Her discourse seemed to have neither beginning nor end but poured forth, spring-fed, an unending stream. Polite and attentive at first, Reuben and Spring were soon offering varied excuses for their departure. Micah, Mrs. F.'s sole hired hand, a short, weather-beaten man of indeterminate age who ate with them at table, had already learned the fine art of tuning her out.

It seemed Mrs. F's late husband had been a paragon of virtue, a man of taste, discernment, learning, and hard work. He'd appreciated Mrs. Flemming's many fine quantities, and despite working from sunup to sundown had taken the time to show that appreciation. Hard work she urged upon her listeners also, with the appreciation sure to follow.

For almost a week, as semi-permanent guests of Mrs. F, they'd waited for Mike Forester to arrange for an escort to take them to Flagstaff. "You can't go alone. Those Indians from the Canyon are out there waiting, you can be sure." Perhaps the Havasupai were waiting; and perhaps they had returned to the Canyon. Rubin planned to ride out that morning and make his own recognizance.

Spring had appeared at breakfast in the skirt and blouse she'd worn to the barn dance the night before. The sleeves were long and bell-shaped at the wrists, with Spring's small and shapely fingers barely visible at the ends. Mrs. Flemming suggested Spring might want to change her clothes before settling down to work—an unnecessary reminder Reuben thought, but Spring had only smiled warmly and asked if she might help serve the morning meal.

When Helen appeared, late, in a short-sleeved blouse that showed off her arms, she was as filled with chatter as she had been the evening before and the two women—Helen and Mrs. Flemming, one old, one young, soon dominated the conversation. Mrs. Flemming seemed captivated by the young girl, declaring her "the daughter I never had," and offering to improve her dress with pins, a spray of flowers, and even a fine lace shawl to all of which Helen responded in a gracious and grateful way that only doubled Mrs. Flemming's devotion.

Reuben and Micah the hired hand were dispatched early to the fields, though Reuben protested he was really better at working with animals. "We've already a blacksmith," Mrs. Fleming replied as if shoeing a horse had been what Reuben had in mind.

Reuben was given a pair of homemade leather boots, the late Mr. F's, and offered the use of a shirt and a hat, "if he wanted them." He accepted the shirt that his own might be washed; the new shirt of rough cotton was homemade and had already been patched once or twice. Mr. Flemming's hat he set aside after Spring and Helen giggled when he tried it on.

Spring was given the washing and the ironing to do along with a further reminder that she might want to change her clothing. Helen, for some reason, was excused from chores. "You're like the daughter I never had," Mrs. Flemming said for the fourteenth time, and so Helen was able to spend most of the morning following in Mrs. Flemming's footsteps, prattling about the previous night's dance, while Mrs. Flemming, herself, labored tirelessly.

Reuben was willing to give Mrs. Flemming credit for her hard work. And credit too for her cooking. It was the unceasing flow of advice and admonitions that he could have done without. Fortunately, Micah was quiet company and the day a particularly pleasant one. Reuben felt that, together, he and Micah did a good morning's work, not only thoroughly weeding a long neglected field—a tiresome chore he'd avoided since he was a teenager, but mending a fence and excavating a tree stump. He was ready for the meal of beef and fresh bread and relish and new potatoes with iced herb tea and apple cider Mrs. Flemming and Helen brought out to the two men at noon.

Mrs. Flemming talked at them while they ate this ample lunch, talked continuously as she had that morning, though insisting they "relax and take the time to do her cooking justice." As she had just finished criticizing the quantity and quality of their morning's work, Micah and Reuben took this latter admonition with a grain of salt. Mrs. F's own hands remained busy with darning that she'd brought from the house. These were large hands, big and rough as Mrs. Flemming herself, with huge dough-like fingers, though to hear Mrs. Flemming talk she was still the simple slip of a girl, not much bigger about the waist then Helen, "that little dear," that Mr. Flemming had married and brought with him west from St Louis.

"St Louis! Oh, tell me about St Louis," said Helen and the two women exchanged memories, the one of a busy but comfortable young adulthood in the home of a busy hostler, the other of a short six-week period in St Louis which it seemed was all the memory of a white world Helen had left to her, that and the memory of a father who had hugged her, a younger brother who had died in a fire, and a new and still younger brother who remained with her mother back in the Indian village in the Canyon.

"You poor girl; you poor girl," Mrs. Fleming would say, and urge Helen to go back to the house and lie down, "this instant," while in the same breath she'd turn on Reuben and Micah and point out the sad quality of their morning's efforts: How this root was still partially in the ground and would have to be got at and removed even if they "had to dig to China," of where the stumps were to be dragged for drying before being chopped for firewood—"a horse? you think you need a horse? Why Mr. Flemming would no more use a horse for such work than he would teach a horse arithmetic"—and of how the hoeing was to be done proper, "unless they planned to spend that entire autumn picking at the weeds they'd missed."

"She tells you to relax, she tells you to get busy. Like my mom," Reuben said under his breath.

"She's got other ideas, if you ask me," whispered Micah cryptically. And perhaps Mrs. F had. "You're a brawny lad," she said to Reuben more than once, admiring the turn of his shoulders, "like Mr. Flemming himself.

"And you've got good manners. Doesn't he have good manners, dear?"

"Yes," said Helen thoughtfully, "though sometimes he belches after a meal."

"Well, never you mind about that. That's a sign a man folk likes your cooking. Do you like my cooking, Mr. Lee?"

"Very much," Reuben said politely, "I've not tasted food this good in New Orleans."

"A flatterer," she said coquettishly. "Best cook in the town, Mr Flemming told me many a time and that's when we were back in St Louis.

"I like a man who likes his food," she said and struck Reuben a smashing blow on the arm. Though intended for a love pat, the blow smarted long after she was gone.

"I think she likes you," Micah said quietly after they were alone again in the field. Reuben gave him a sharp look. Micah had barely said two words to Reuben all that morning and that he spoke at all was significant.

"What do you mean likes me?" Reuben said and rubbed his arm where Mrs. Flemming had struck him. He waited, but apparently Micah had said his piece. "Maybe so. Maybe she thinks I'm just like the son she never had."

"Thinks you're just like her next husband," Micah said, putting his words down one at a time like chops with an ax.

"You're crazy," but Reuben had occasion to recall Micah's words that afternoon when Mrs. Flemming contrived on more than one flimsy pretext to visit them in the fields. "Husband?" he said to himself, "to her?"

Towards four o'clock, when Mike appeared at the Flemming farm on horseback, Reuben had a second reason for apprehension. "They've burned down the Westin place," Mike said.

"Was anyone hurt?" Reuben asked. He did not have to be told who "they" were.

"No. Fortunately, both Mr. and Mrs. Westin were in town for the dance. They live out to the east of town, north of where you said you rode in. House, barn, everything was on fire. Too late to do anything. The Westins just had to sit there and watch it burn. Good thing too. You see, Dick Westin was all for riding in and saving the animals. But his wife says no, he'll just get hurt in the fire. Then, while they're arguing, she thinks she sees someone sneaking around in the bushes. Turns out she saved both their lives by telling him to wait. They watch where she's pointing and are able to make out a half dozen Injuns hidden back in the shadows just waiting to gather scalps.

"Not one or two Indians either; they say they saw a whole gang of them hiding out there. The Westins hid in the shadows themselves until dawn and then circled back. Somebody only thought to tell me an hour ago."

"What about the other farms?" Reuben wanted to know.

"I've sent some of the boys out to all of them, telling the people to head back in toward town. No way we can protect them all but if we stay together. How many Injuns did you say there were?"

Reuben thought for a minute. "Nine, ten, maybe a dozen at most. And I think I wounded a couple. Killed one too, I'm pretty sure."

"Well, Dick says there were at least twenty. Dick may be excitable, but he and his wife had all night to count 'em."

"Where'd the other Indians come from?" Reuben asked. He had a feeling he already knew the answer: the original party of warriors had been supplemented by a better-equipped, better-supplied expedition from the Canyon.

"That's what I'd like to know."

Although Mike had ridden out to the field directly, deliberately bypassing the house to avoid a long discussion, Mrs. Flemming soon came rushing up with Helen in tow to find out what was going on. "Just seeing how Mr. Lee was doing," Mike lied, "you seem to have got yourself a pretty good worker."

"Good enough," Mrs. F said, "though I'm afraid that shiftless Micah may be teaching him bad habits."

"I was thinking of going into town with Mike tomorrow," Reuben said innocently. "I'm afraid we may have put him and some others in town to a great deal of trouble. I'd like to give him a hand, pay our way."

"Yes," Mike said glibly, "Someone's got to help the Stewart's fix their wall... their shed."

Mrs. F gave them a fixed unwavering stare that brought Mike's glibness to a halt. "You're not a very good liar, Mike Forester. Nor are you Reuben Lee. Just like the first Mr. Flemming. Now, you Mike Forester, what's is going on?"

Mike tried to tell her briefly. "Oh God, we'll all be murdered in our beds," Mrs. F began, before Mike had completed half a dozen sentences. Seeing Helen's face, she switched her tone in mid sentence, .".. if it weren't for these good men to protect us. And shouldn't Mr. Lee be staying here to protect her, us from harm?"

"I sort of feel responsible," said Reuben.

"You've responsibilities here," snapped Mrs. F.

Reuben said nothing. Finally, Mrs. F reached out and touched his arm. "Well if you must go dear, you must."

"I'll change my clothes," Reuben said as he began to walk back toward the house. Helen followed immediately, taking his hand in hers, "Oh, Reuben, you're so brave."

"Now hold on dear, wait for me," Mrs. F called, puffing in her heavy clothing as she raced to catch up with the others.

Only Micah was left in the field to lean thoughtfully on his hoe and wonder, not for the first time, how she expected him to get anything done if she would assign him ten tasks at once and then assign him ten more before the first ten were complete.

"Now Mike Forester, you wait up for me," Mrs. Flemming said when they'd returned to the house. Reuben had already disappeared inside.

"Surely, Mrs. F, just you lean against old Reliant here."

"I'm not tired," she said, "I'm just a little out of breath. Now Mike, you just can't come in here and walk off with Mr. Lee because you want to play at cowboys and Indians. I've got a farm to run here."

"I'm hardly dragging him away," Mike said. "He just feels he ought to go."

"What if he gets killed? I don't know him very well you know. What if he gets killed before we've had a chance to know each other better? I've already lost one man, you know Mike."

"Doesn't Reuben already have a squaw?"

"A squaw doesn't really count as a wife does she?" she said imploringly. It was clear the older woman was lonely and hoping for another male companion. Mike, who knew Reuben's strong feelings about Helen, did not reply.

That evening, Mrs. F came to Reuben's room, a curtain-screened alcove off to the side of the kitchen and knocked on the adjoining wall. "Mr. Lee, are you decent? May I come in?

When she arrived, Reuben was lying on his back on the coverlet, his boots still on. Quickly, he swung his feet over the side. He grinned, embarrassed, "I shouldn't have had my feet on the bed."

"No," Mrs. F said with a sour expression, "Perhaps, we should have you sleep outside with the hired." Then, as if she realized she might have gone too far, she replaced the angry look with a sort of idiotic grin, like an angelic cat trying to charm a mouse out of its hole.

"I found something," she said, "which I thought might interest you, Mr. Lee, being as you're from the big city, New Orleans and all." Reuben tried to protest, "just a farm upriver," but Mrs. F's attention was completely focused on the object she was unwrapping, perhaps for the first time since she'd come out West from St Louis.

The object was an exquisite piece of porcelain, a white bowl with blue borders and a line of blue charioteers that raced endlessly around a circular course along its outer rim. "It's Greek," she said, "It's an exact copy of an ancient Greek bowl. My father gave it to me. He was a minister. See how it gleams, how it captures the light?"

"It's very beautiful," Reuben said.

"I have some other beautiful things," she continued. "Would you like to see them?"

"Perhaps, Helen and Spring would like to see them, too."

"Oh, it's no trouble. I can show *them* another time. We're together now."

She showed him another bowl and a mug with a bust of a man's head on the front of it that she called a Toby jug, and the bonnet she said she'd worn just after she and Mr. F were married, and a long formal dress with gold threads in the hem.

"They're all very beautiful, Mrs. F," Reuben said.

"They come with the house," she replied and smiled bashfully. She turned red, then redder and then, finally, grabbing up her possessions, she scurried from the room.

Reuben lay back on the coverlet, expecting his thoughts would again turn to the Havasupai circling the town, but instead he found himself poised on the lip of the Canyon like an eagle, soaring across its lofty spires, following a downdraft to spiral lower and lower past granite and sandstone through a billion years of history until, somewhere in his flight, but long before the eagle had settled on the canyon floor, he fell asleep.

Chapter 10

The next morning, the arguments began all over again, with Mrs. Flemming trying to take both sides simultaneously, whichever would suit her needs. First, she said they would need Reuben at the farm in case the Indians attacked. But when Helen worried aloud about the attack coming while Reuben was out working in the fields, Mrs. Flemming told her not to be concerned: "I've got a shotgun and I can make good use of it. Mr. F has taught me how. You don't need to fret."

Reuben took no part in the arguments. The decision had already been made for him years ago by his father and uncles. A man did his duty, no if's and's nor but's, no running from one's fears.

As soon as he'd finished all of the second stack of pancakes that Mrs. F set before him, he slipped out of the dining room and set about checking over his clothing. Mr. F's clothes were not at all the correct size. Mr. F had dined too well on Mrs. F's cooking—Reuben had a brief vision of the humpty-dumpty-like pair pushing against each other, while Reuben, though his waist was now hard with muscle, was still as thin as he'd been when a teenager. He took a curry brush to his own worn pants and did his best to render them soft and clean again. He took advantage a second time of the hot water and Mr. F's razor so that when he ventured back into the parlor all the women agreed he looked "handsome."

"Be careful." Helen told him. Spring gave him a brief hug and told him not to worry about her and Helen. "I can shoot a gun, too, you know, that is, if Mrs. F has one for me."

"I'm,... I'm not sure dear. About giving you a gun that is." Mrs. Flemming's face was distorted. It was clear what she was thinking without her actually saying it out loud: Spring had to be some kind of Indian and you didn't give an Indian a gun. No sense arguing with Mrs. Flemming about it, Reuben realized, and began to remove his own gun from its holster. Spring probably wouldn't need it. The Indians hadn't attacked so far. They probably wouldn't until they'd had a chance to parley with the town leaders. But it was best to be on the safe side. And after the parley? He was not so sure.

Spring pushed away his gun. "I'm not an Indian, Mrs. F. And no, I'm not a Mexican either. I'm Spanish, the daughter of the Spanish ambassador. I was kidnapped by the Indians just as Helen was."

"It's true Mrs. F," cried Helen and she threw her arms about her friend, looking as fierce as Reuben could ever remember Helen looking which was not very fierce at all. Apparently, Mrs. F also was touched by Helens's loyalty to Spring. "Spanish," Mrs. F said; "Well then, maybe it's all right. I guess I could find a gun for her." But on thinking this development over Mrs. F gave both Reuben and Spring a sour look. If the girl wasn't an Indian, what did this mean about the relationship between her and Reuben?

He met Mike on the porch outside of Mike's mercantile. "Looks like you've got a new admirer," Mike said, alluding to Mrs. F, as he and Reuben rode out of town.

"She's old enough to be my mother," Reuben snapped, "and don't you tell me that I'm old enough to be somebody else's you know what."

"My lips are sealed, Reuben. But all the same, Mrs. F is just forty-four. She's a hard worker and the best cook in the valley. I lied about Mrs. Stewart the other day. You could do worse, if you stayed. Less you're partial to Mexicans or Spanish, or whatever they call themselves."

"Maybe I am," said Reuben. And for a moment Spring's face— the large, intense eyes, the full mouth and black gold hair, and

Helen's kitten-like visage, and the face of Helen's mother, the way she'd been that day in the Canyon walking with pride through the Indian village all blurred together before him.

Outside of Mike's house, which was set adjacent to the store which Mike owned, a bewhiskered gentleman was standing, one hand resting lightly on the back of a beat-up looking Indian pony. He wore Indian moccasins rather than boots, and cloth leggings over long leather trousers.

"Clem! I'm glad you came," Mike said. "This is Clem," he said to Reuben enthusiastically.

"Overland express, retired," Clem said. "Clem is a prospector," Mike said.

"From California?" Reuben asked.

"No, he's been looking for gold right here, in these hills."

"Five years now," said Clem.

"But..." Reuben began, meaning to finish by saying, "I didn't know there was any gold here."

"None of your but's sonny. I know there's gold in California; I also know there's gold here, gold I won't have to share with nobody."

"But where..." Reuben began again.

"Don't ask him that," said Mike, "Clem's sensitive about that."

"Don't ask me where, sonny. Cause I ain't a goin to tell you. Ain't a goin t'share the gold with anybody."

Reuben looked at Clem, no taller than the pony, beard filthy and tobacco-stained, teeth missing or mere stumps, but said nothing.

"I know what you're thinking," Clem said, "I ain't no better than an Indian. Well, I ain't the one who's got the squaw."

"She's not my squaw," Reuben protested.

"Clem's the best Indian guide we've got," said Mike quickly, changing the subject.

"You mean the only one stupid enough to parley with a Havasupai war party."

"You know their language?" Reuben said surprised.

"You bet I do." Clem made a series of guttural sounds that Reuben did not recognize.

"Know what I said?" the old man asked.

"No, I... "

"I said 'I like the looks of your wife. I want to sleep with her.' These Indians trade wives a lot," he confided unnecessarily and, Reuben thought, leaping inwardly to Spring's defense, falsely.

"We'll ride out to their camp now," Mike said, "If that's all right with you Clem?"

"A parley is what I came to town for."

The three men said little as they rode out of town in the direction of where the Westin ranch had once stood. Reuben thought of its probable appearance now, a cluster of burnt-out buildings with maybe a section of green lumber standing roofless in one corner. I bring trouble wherever I go, Reuben thought morosely, wherever people are.

"I like your horse," Clem said to him breaking the silence. "Fine animal. Good bottom. What's his name?"

"Champion. He is a fine horse. He's a Morgan. Traded almost two months wages for him and 'twas well worth of it."

"Indians may like him too. Are you ready to trade?"

A cold chill went through Reuben's body. Trade Champion? He remembered when he'd first bought the small Morgan and the comments on his size. He remembered the roping contest they'd won together back before Champion had a permanent name. The other horse was larger and faster, but Champion and he were still working smoothly, powerfully long after the other horse and rider were winded. Trade Champion for Helen? If it had to be, it had to be.

"Guess, I best go talk to them, then." Clem pressed a spur into his pony's flank and the two disappeared quickly over the rise.

"Bastard," Reuben said when he'd ridden off.

"He will have his fun," Mike said. "Indians don't eat horses do they?"

Mike turned serious. "Reuben, is there anything I don't know? Anything you should tell me? We're going to have to make some decisions here. Decisions that may affect the whole town."

Reuben wasn't sure what Mike was getting at, but he told him the whole story again from start to finish. The discovery of the Winstons in the village at the bottom of the Canyon. His talk with Helen that first night by the river. The exchange of blankets between Circling Owl and Helen's adopted father. The theft of the horse and pony on the day they'd escaped from the Canyon. Mike said nothing; he just let all the information soak in as if he were checking through a shipment of hardware for his store.

They heard Clem before they saw him, cussing as he rode over the rise. "Well you sure got a bunch of mad Indians.

"You take one chief's adopted daughter. You take the other chief's daughter-in-law to be. You steal the dowry and their fastest pony. Oh, and if that ain't enough, you walk away with this subchief's concubine who the first chief is planning to take into his own tent."

Was this Spring or Helen he was talking about, Reuben wondered. Chief's concubine? This wasn't what Spring had told him.

"Forget it Clem," Mike said, "Reuben's already told me about that hisself. How's it look?"

"How's it look? It looks bad. Depends on how fast the army gets here whether we all die or a few of us gets away."

"We're not helpless, Clem. A few like you and me and Reuben here can shoot a mean gun. Far as I can see, we have twice the Indian's manpower. But I know what you mean. I sent a man to the army in Flagstaff day before yesterday."

"Cawdry?"

"Yep."

"Wouldn't count on it." Clem spat on the ground. "I'm pretty sure they got him. I didn't let on I know as much of their language as I do."

"Damn, Cawdry was a good man." Mike turned his head away from them for a moment, "Could we trade them? Give them something to make up for their loss?

"I know you were joking about Reuben's horse, but we could give em back their ponies—that O.K. with you, Reuben?"

"Sure, I never intended to get you all in trouble."

"No bother. You did the only thing a white man could have done once you realized they had white women as prisoners."

"Give them the girl," Clem began.

"Helen, never!" a shrill boy/man's voice rang out from behind them. Frank, the dark haired youth from the barn dance the night before, shook one clenched fist in the air. And behind him Mrs. Flemming and Tom and one or two other people from the town stood together in a worried group.

"What are you doing here?" Mike challenged.

"We come to stand up for Helen," Frank said and the others behind him nodded.

"I'll take care of Helen," Reuben said.

"You? Old man." Frank made 'old' sound like another word for 'corpse.'

"We're not going to fight among ourselves," Mike said.

"Them Injuns can smell quarreling," Clem said, "Same as a coyote knows enough to pick out the injured member of a herd."

I'm losing Helen, Reuben thought, either way. Whether she goes back with the Indians or stays here with one of the younger men. "Would the Indians take me?" he asked Clem.

"Don't be silly," Mike said. "You're no Indian's slave. No white man is. We'll give them something else."

"No!" shouted Mrs. Flemming, "I've already lost the one man."

"Well, Helen's not going back," said Frank.

"She won't have to go back," said Mike, "This is all just silly. We'll ride out and talk to the Indians, just Reuben and Clem and me. See what we can trade em. Horses, yes. Food, maybe some farm tools. But not people. They've got to learn that, even if they've got to learn it from a gun."

"We'll have to leave our guns," Clem said.

"What!"

"That's what I arranged. A peace parley. Three of us. Three of them. No guns, no tomahawks."

"One of us should have a rifle," Mike said.

"You want the fighting to begin now?"

"I've brought the horses," said Mrs. F. "Spring suggested I bring them." The big Bay with its single white stocking and the powerful little pony that Helen loved were led into the clearing. "Might be a good idea, if we added another horse or two," said Clem. Frank got down from his gelding, slapped the animal's rump and sent him forward after the other horses. Not believing what he was doing,

Reuben slipped off Champion and stood beside him on the ground prepared to send him forward also.

"Best you ride him till we get there, don't you think," said Clem to Reuben.

"We've got other horses," said Mike, looking to the others.

"I want them to have my horse," announced Frank.

"I'll..." began Reuben.

"You'll do what you're told this one time," said Mike. "Get back up."

"Yes, Sir."

The negotiators met finally in a hollow between two ridges. In Reuben's mind, the scene would be impressed forever against a field of dried yellow flowers, their wind-blown petals loose upon the ground. Reuben could not remember having passed through this hollow on the flight to Sojurn, though he marked the passage of many horses through it in the past. In the very center of the narrow valley stood three Indians, among them Circling Hawk, the one who had come so close to killing him during the long chase.

"Don't show fear," Mike said, unnecessarily, which showed how much fear Mike must be feeling himself. Mike hung back at their rear, the mirror image of the old Havasupai warrior who brought up the tail of the Indians' party of three.

Circling Owl was in the middle of his party, bare-chested. His reddish-brown skin was covered with markings including two long cuts that had been made freshly with a knife. He wore the same buckskin leggings he had worn on the trail, over not under his moccasins. He carried no weapons—no knife, no tomahawk, no signs of bow and arrow, only a long empty tube in the belt around his waist.

The battered face of the Indian at the front of the party showed the scars of many battles. His face had been carefully painted that morning with thin white lines. According to Clem, these markings said that he had come to parley, not to make war. If other Indians remained hidden up on the ridge, bow and arrow and rifle trained on the hollow, they were invisible.

The Indian with the battered face stepped forward and waited at the bottom. Reuben walked forward next leading the string of horses until he reached a point about three-quarters of the way down the ridge. As Clem continued forward past him, Reuben tried to hold himself as erect and fearless as Circling Hawk across the way and wondered if Circling Hawk, inside, were equally fearful.

Clem talked with the Indian with the battered face. Both men used their hands and arms as much as their voices. Then the Indian with the battered face moved back and spoke with Circling Hawk. The old warrior in the rear looked as if he were prepared to speak, but he had no opportunity. Circling Hawk had already pounded the backside of his own horse and begun to shout.

The gift was refused. A translation was unnecessary and, indeed, Clem did not bother to translate what had been said. "He wants Helen," Clem said on his return.

"No," Reuben said.

"Thought, you'd say that."

"Tell him, he can have me as a slave."

"I don't think you'd want to do that," said Clem.

"Tell him," Reuben demanded.

An exchange of words in Havasupai between Clem and the Indian with the battered face followed. Circling Hawk voiced a series of guttural sounds. Clem translated, finally, "He says you'll be his slave all right, after they burn down the town."

Reuben shook his fist. In an instant Circling Owl had darted forward, hands upraised. The oldest of the Indians, silent until now, barked a command. The Indian with the battered face threw his arms about Circling Owl and was dragged forward after him, heels digging into the ground.

Gradually, Reuben became conscious of Clem's hand on his own arm, pulling him back. Reuben, too, had moved forward instinctively, ready to engage in combat.

"Not now," hissed Clem, "we'll lose face."

"I'll kill him now," said Reuben.

"You won't and he won't," said Clem. "We'll talk to Mike, first. Asides, moving back to talk to Mike will take us farther away from them Indians."

"I thought they had no weapons," Reuben said.

"Maybe they don't, but I believe they can get to them fast enough.

"If I was you," Clem said to Mike when he and Reuben had come abreast of the other man, "I'd shoot them now and parley later."

"But we didn't bring any guns. You said not to," Mike stammered.

"What I said, and what you ought to have done are two different things," said Clem. "They want Helen and they want the horses and they want this man's scalp. And since we ain't gonna give em to em, we might as well be the ones that start the shooting."

"They want Spring Morning, too, I suppose," Mike said wryly. He hadn't intended the question seriously, just as something to say while he decided on a course of action, but Clem was not one for subtlety.

"Nahh, I asked them about that," Clem said, spitting on the ground and adding further color to the soil. "They said we could keep the half breed." Clem laughed, "Seems like them Injuns got the same kind of prejudice 'gainst Mexicans that we do."

"Spanish, she's Spanish," Reuben said inanely.

"No matter," said Clem, "I suggest we smile at the Injuns as if we agreed with everythin' they wants and then ride the hell out of here." He turned to Mike, "You sent to Flagstaff for the Army right?"

"I sent a second man this morning," Mike said. "Much good it will do us," said Clem. "We'll have killing before dawn tomorry."

Chapter 11

Shortly after dawn the next morning, the Havasupai attacked, a rain of arrows on the settlers' headquarters that landed harmlessly for the most part. They then set about riding from one end of the valley to the other, shooting and burning as they went.

The plan that Mike Forester had pieced together the previous evening might have worked had the townspeople been an army, or had the settlers had time to drill and work out the details of his plan, or had there even been more of a general agreement about the danger the Indians presented.

Too many of the settlers remained in their own homes instead of joining the others at the agreed-upon gathering place. Many of these fought bravely even when attacked at overwhelming odds. But their absence only weakened the main force. The Indians would try for a quick kill, destroying all resistance, then setting the home and barn on fire. If they met with too much opposition, they would simply ride on, only to return later with redoubled numbers when the householders thought the danger was past.

Had the settlers been trained in the arts of war, they would have followed on the heels of the retreating Indians, harrying and attacking them from behind even as the Indians met with fresh opposition from in front. But the settlers were not trained soldiers, but civilians; they remained in their homes, content with their isolated victory, lost in a glow of premature congratulation, while the attacking horde moved on probing for the next weak spot.

The old Russian fable—Tolstoy repeats it in his book of stories for children, compares the members of a family, or the citizens of a town like Sojurn with the straws in a broomstick: united they can withstand all opposition, separate, they are easily broken.

When the Indians returned—and it seemed as if the Havasupai always returned, that they would give the settlers no respite till the town of Sojurn was completely destroyed—they came with double their original numbers. One by one they picked off the sharpshooters, while a rain of fire arrows forced the settlers to abandon their fortified positions.

The death of their comrades did not seem to deter the Havasupai, while the settlers keened deeply over each loss. A farmer's wife who could shoot every bit as straight and as accurately as her husband would be assigned to tend the injured; another settler might stop firing to hug a frightened child. The Indians abandoned their own wounded, and the abandoned braves fought on to the death.

Mike's one contribution, a system of riders on horseback who carried the news of the Havasupai attacks from one part of the town to another, turned out to be the settlers' final undoing. A man would come riding up to Mike's headquarters, shouting the news, "They're attacking the Smith place." Someone would remember that Smith had once loaned him a plow or given him a hand with his animals when he was sick, another that he was Smith's second cousin. And the two men would ride off toward the Smith's, further fragmenting the group.

The times of quiet were as or more dangerous than the times of action. Now came a moment for reflection and for fear. Some wife would remember, "Oh Tom, we've gone and left that sampler your mother gave us." Tom would say, "Well, it's quiet now. I'll just ride out to the farm and see if I can't sneak out the sampler before those thieving redskins get to it." Had Mike been a captain and Tom a private, he would have ordered Tom to stay put, gun at the ready, and do his job. But he wasn't and Tom wasn't, and so Tom rode off, to be gone still when the redskins returned to the attack.

By noon, the townspeople knew the army wasn't coming. The settlers had allowed themselves to be divided into three small groups, or maybe it was five, it depended on whether you counted one man left by himself, leg broken and twisted under him, squatting in a burning building with his rifle on his knees. The only decision Mike had left to make was whether to send another rider off in the direction of Flagstaff, another rider who would arrive too late, who would only report the complete destruction of the town.

Chapter 12

"Let them know how few of us are left." Mike said.

Reuben pulled his own tired body erect. "Shall I come back when I've given them the message?"

Mike stared blankly at the wall for a few moments. Somewhere, deep inside the mountain, the settling of the earth had undermined this rocky crag. The voice that emerged, finally, seemed to belong to someone else. "No. Stay there and help them if you can. Or go, just go Reuben."

Come with me, Reuben wanted to shout. But Mike remained slumped against the wall, every aspect of his body registering defeat. In an hour or so the Indians would return. Mike would kill a few more of them before he died—Mike was a very brave man, but in the end he would die as all the others around him had died.

And it's all my fault.

The Paltry farm, just on the edge of town, housed the only other buildings that were still standing. These too had seen the fire arrows. But the flames had been extinguished, the buildings saved. At a cost of how many lives, Reuben wondered.

He found Helen, finally, eyes wild and hair tangled, looking much the way she must have looked when she was ten, the day the Comanche had attacked the wagon train that housed her family, the day she'd seen her father killed, and watched helpless as she and her mother were driven off into slavery.

Spring Morning sat next to Helen in one corner of what had once been a tool shed. Four dead men sat near them still clutching their rifles. Mrs. Flemming's body was on the path outside just a few yards from the doorway. She had been running toward the shed, rifle in hand, when she was struck from behind. Her scalp had been removed.

"I've tried to get Helen to lie down," Spring said to him. "You must drink something darling," she said to Helen and handed her the dipper of water. Helen drank from the dipper, gulping down the water as if she were an animal rather than a human being. Her eyes were glazed over and staring straight ahead.

"She's so young," Spring Morning said, "She's never really grown up since she was captured." For the first time, Reuben noticed how young Helen really was. Her pretty unlined face, without the eyes to give it intelligence, was helpless, childlike.

"You're coming with me," he said, "both of you." He picked Helen up in his arms and motioned for Spring to follow with the water bags. No point in them staying around any longer. The town was burned, the surrounding farms destroyed. Dead Indians and whites lay everywhere.

He could no longer avoid facing up to the fact: It was he, Reuben, who had come and brought destruction to the town, who brought bad luck with him wherever he rode.

"Frank?" Helen said unexpectedly. Reuben bent over her to be sure he could hear her faint words. "Frank?" she asked.

"No. It's Reuben."

"I thought it might be Frank. Have you seen Frank?"

"No."

"He said he was going to ride out to the farm today."

"I think she's hallucinating," Spring said.

"No I'm not. It was just the Indians came before Frank got here."

"She doesn't remember the ride into town," Spring explained.

"Yes I do," Helen murmured, her eyes half shut, her voice no more than a whisper. "We came here and Mrs. Flemming said not to worry, 'I was just like the daughter she never had.' She had a rifle and a pitchfork and she and Micah went to sit by the horses. They told Spring to stay with me. They gave Spring a rifle because she's such a good shot. And they gave me a gun too."

"You made them," Spring said.

"I made them. And we could hear the shooting and smell the smoke far, far away long before the Havasupai came. They killed Micah and Mr. Stewart. And Mrs. Flemming. I saw them cut her scalp right off her head.

"Circling Owl came for me then, the way he said he would. He came right to the door of the shed. He knocked and when it wouldn't open, he blew on it. I shot him. I shot Circling Owl. Didn't I Spring Morning?"

"No, you didn't," Spring answered too quickly.

"I shot him right through the window. He's dead."

"Oh Helen. You did not shoot him. Have some more water and then sleep, sleep."

"Not now," said Reuben, sliding his hands under Helen's light frame and preparing to pick her up a second time if she could not stand on her own, "She'll have to stay awake. We don't have time. We'll start walking. Do you know where your horses are?"

"I know where they were," Spring said.

The threesome circled warily until they found where Spring's horse and Helen's pony had been tethered with the other horses away from the barn and under the trees. Miraculously, the Bay and the Pinto were still there feeding quietly on a bale of hay. So, too, were the bodies of the two Indians who had come to claim them and been shot by Micah or Mrs. Flemming for their audacity.

"They put us off in the tool shed where we would be out of the way," said Spring, "I told them I could shoot, but they did not listen.

'Good, take care of Helen.' they said. Everybody is very fond of Helen."

Helen said nothing; though she seemed to be sleeping against Reuben's shoulder her breath came and went unevenly as though she were stopping and starting continually, reliving over and over the same event. "Helen did shoot one of the Indians. Would you believe it. And she didn't even know how to hold the gun. Not Circling Owl though. Wise Moon. He was not particularly brave. Not much of a farmer either. Just sort of someone who was there. He was always nice to me. He told funny stories."

One of the horses lay on the ground, its leg bent underneath it. A second horse, similar in color, stood near its fallen comrade whinnying in sympathy with the first horse's pain. "I've got to shoot this horse," Reuben said. "We'll walk away; put Helen down on some soft ground, gently, so she won't wake up. I'll come back, shoot the horse, then we'll go. Get your Bay and the pony now."

They rode in silence until they had returned to Reuben's original post. No one was left alive. Even Clem, indefatigable, had died at last, victim of both arrow and knife. The Indians had ridden away finally, satisfied with the destruction they had wrought; no sound of them to be heard. "Which direction are you going?" Spring asked.

Reuben looked up at the afternoon sun and thought for the first time about where he was going, about where they were all going to go. They could not make it to Flagstaff as Mike had wanted; the Indians held the Northern route all the way from there to the Canyon. "South," he said, "We'll go south. To Mexico maybe." He smiled as if this were a private joke that only Spring and he shared. She found herself smiling back. "But we'll head west first," he said, putting an arm around her waist and pointing to the afternoon sun.

Spring squinted. "You can't see if anyone is out there," she said.

"I know. But once we're farther west, they won't be able to see us from here against the sun. It will be a calculated risk when we start out. They may see us then. But I don't think they will." He'd finished harnessing the animals by that time, splitting the remaining saddlebags and water between Spring's Bay and Helen's pony. He swung Helen up light as a feather to his own saddle and then climbed behind her. "Just at first," he said to Spring.

Nobody fired at them. Behind them the town burned. Even when they had gone perhaps four hours and twenty miles, they could still see the faint pall of gray smoke hanging in the sky over where the town had been.

The trip west then south from Sojurn was as bad as their flight from the Canyon had been. In some ways it was worse. Fleeing the Canyon, they'd had hope. Find a settlement of white men, rest, then go on. Now, only terror lay behind them and they could take little comfort in what lay ahead. California? Mexico? They might as well be heading for the moon.

When the sun went down, they halted, even though some light remained in the sky. "We need sleep," he said, "All of us."

"I'm not arguing," Spring replied. "May I sleep near you?"

"Sure."

"I mean I..."

He put his hand on her shoulder as if to say, "that's all right," and she immediately slumped against him. She's worn out, he thought, we all are.

He had meant to stay awake, with Helen against one shoulder and Spring on the other, watching while the moon sailed overhead and then down into the trees, but his eyes closed too, lids as heavy as two iron bars, lids impossible to open. Long before the time he'd intended to wake Spring to take the next watch he was asleep.

It did not matter; the Havasupai had not pursued them. When he awoke, sleeping with his arms about Helen, slowly conscious of the weight removed from his other arm, the sky overhead was pitch black. He could hear their horses moving about in the trees nearby. And someone else moving nearby as well!

"It's all right," Spring whispered, bending over him and running a finger over his lips to keep him from speaking in reply.

"Thirsty. I'm thirsty," he said.

"I know, I got up to give Helen some water. We're all thirsty." She handed him the dipper.

"Helen? How's Helen?" He seemed to have forgotten she was sleeping next to him.

"She's quiet, maybe a little feverish."

"I was going to wake you, have you watch while I slept."

"A little late for that," Spring chuckled. "But I was watching. Now I'd like to sleep some more."

"I'll watch," Reuben said.

When the dawn came, he was still watching, though he had been drifting in and out of sleep for hours. He had thought once of waking Spring to relieve him, but she too was sleeping so peacefully, that he had let her lay, nestled against him, her head on one saddlebag. "Water," Helen moaned.

"I'll get you water," he said.

Chapter 13

When Spring awoke, about an hour after the sun had risen, they discovered Helen was burning up with fever.

"What's wrong?" Reuben asked.

"I don't know. She may have caught a chill. She's hurt her shoulder, too. When the gun went off.

"She needs a medicine man, Reuben."

"Doctor," Reuben substituted.

"Or a doctor. We're a long way from both." Spring thought for a minute, "The leaves of the trees are supposed to be good for fever."

"Do you know which leaves?"

"I know what they're supposed to smell like."

He set about collecting a sample of leaves, one from each tree in the area. Some Spring discarded at once, others she crushed between her fingers. She found the right type, finally, and brewed a strong smelling batch of dark tea that they fed to Helen over her feeble protests.

"Do you think it helped?" Reuben asked

"She drank it all," Spring said. "And didn't it smell awful." She giggled. Reuben snorted and they both began to laugh. "Oh my," Spring said after awhile, "Did we wake her?" But Helen slept peacefully. Perhaps something in the leaves had calmed her. Her fever seemed lower too, so that after breakfast, they started off toward the south again.

As Champion appeared able to bear the double weight with ease, Reuben kept Helen with him in the saddle. I like the feel of her against me, he said to himself, the smell of her hair. "We'll brew her some more tea, this evening."

But by late afternoon, Helen's fever was worse. They did not know whether to stop and tend to her or continue riding in the vain hope they would reach a settlement. He held Helen close to him but the names she cried out in her fever, "Frank" and "Circling Hawk," were not his own. Her face was very pale. It seemed to him her chest barely moved when she breathed. I want you to get better, he prayed.

Despite the risk of detection, they stopped, made a fire, and brewed Helen another cup of the leaf tea. Again she drank it, again she fell asleep, and again, it seemed to them, her fever subsided. When the evening meal was ready to be eaten, they woke her and tried to feed her, but she showed no interest in the food. She drank more water though and a third cup of the leaf tea, this one warmer and more tempting.

After sunset but before the sunlight had vanished completely from the sky, Reuben carefully strung snares across the surrounding pathways so they would have warning of any intruders. He put out animal snares, too, so that they might have squirrel or rabbit again the next day. The horses seemed content with the grasses available to them in the clearings among the trees.

At breakfast, they rekindled the fire and gave Helen more tea while Reuben tried to puzzle out the absence of pursuit. Clearly, they had entered another tribe's territory, a tribe of which the Canyon Indians were afraid. But which tribe? Arapaho? Digger? Apache? Though Reuben was not skilled at reading Indian signs, he became more and more convinced it was the latter.

When night fell, and Spring Morning gathered more leaves for the tea, Reuben had to make a decision. "What if someone, the Apache, sees our campfire?"

"She'll die else," Spring said and so he built and lit the fire. He salvaged his conscience somewhat by extinguishing the fire thoroughly so that in the morning it was necessary to begin all over again rather than make use of the coals.

"I'm scared," Spring said, as Reuben was bending over Helen for the fourteenth or fifteenth time that evening as if by looking at her face he could will her into good health.

Spring afraid? "Did you get enough to eat?" he asked her.

"I'm frightened Reuben," she said.

"Oh yeah," he said and beckoned to Spring to come closer. He did not want to leave Helen's side. He put an arm around Spring's shoulders and around the shawl she was wearing.

"You can share the shawl," Spring said.

"Oh yeah," Reuben said, letting her adjust it around them both. His arm was directly against her blouse now and he could feel her warmth and smell the light perfume in her hair.

The full moon overhead filled their clearing with a pale silver light. "It would be hard to sleep even if you wanted to," Spring said, putting words to his thoughts. A shooting star streaked across the sky overhead so that she gasped and pressed against him in a mixture of joy and fright. They sat thus until Helen's breathing quieted and slowly became regular and even. Spring's breathing, too, was slow and regular and Reuben saw that she was asleep against his shoulder. Gradually . . . though many of his thoughts were back in Sojurn and he again heard the sound of the guns, felt the heat of the flaming arrows, labored side by side with Bob Stewart and Mike Forester to put out the fires . . . gradually, Reuben, too, fell asleep.

For the next three days, Helen remained in a weakened condition, waking only to be tied to or untied from her horse, or to be dosed with liquids. She drank the water in which they'd cooked their maize and greens, and she took several spoonfuls of a rabbit stew from which they'd removed all the hard-to-chew portions. And, of course, she continued to drink the leaf tea that Spring said was good for her.

Spring had settled on a tea consisting of bark, leaves, fir needles, and some clay soil which was supposed to be good for stomach cramps. Whether this mixture was a great medicine as Spring hoped, or whether Helen, young and in good physical condition, was due for recovery, Helen got better. At least, she got to the point where she wouldn't drink their tea mixture anymore. Sniffing at the discarded cup, Reuben said, "I don't much care for the mixture myself."

The new Helen, still weak, was more reserved than the old. One could tell the loss of her second family back in Sojurn continued to prey on her.

Reuben was happy she was still willing to be held, to have him hold her, and that frequently she would reach up and touch his lips with her lips. When this occurred, he was too absorbed in his newfound love to notice Spring watching them from a distance, pale and reflective. If he'd noticed, he would have known Helen was not the only one who cared for him.

The forest grew thinner; one moment they would be in the shade, the next out in the sunlight again. Because of the risk of detection by the Apache, they made fires only when the sun was up and were careful to select dry wood that would make the minimum of smoke.

Away from the trees, few plants were to be found in the rocky slanted soil as if the rain had long since washed the fertile earth away. The going was easier, faster. In a single day's ride, they equaled the distance they'd traveled in the four days when Helen was sick.

He'd been leading them almost due south through the forest, but now he thought to travel westward again. They did not travel far. Less than a mile from the edge of the forest, the ground ended abruptly in a sheer five hundred foot drop. Beyond that the ground dropped again and again for twenty-five, fifty, a hundred miles it seemed.

They stood for a long while beside the cliff's edge, until the sun had set, with Helen's tiny hand hidden in Reuben's own. Luckily, Spring had the presence of mind to start a fire, to send an unwilling Helen for wood, and to throw the remaining rabbit and squirrel in the pot. When the sun set finally, to the accompaniment of the longest, most incredible painted sunset the three had ever witnessed, warm stew was waiting for empty bellies.

Chapter 14

For some time, they drifted southward, almost aimlessly, letting the contours of the land determine their direction. They encountered no one and saw no signs of pursuit, yet Reuben and Spring became more and more uneasy as it became more and more obvious why the Canyon Indians had not followed them: the signs of the Apache were everywhere.

At first, Reuben and Spring had not wanted to talk about the Apache for fear Helen would overhear and be frightened. But one evening after dark, when they supposed Helen was asleep and still feverish, they began to discuss the Apache in low tones.

They both had heard the tales of unmatched cruelty, of burned disfigured corpses, of prisoners skinned alive. It seemed impossible that Spring herself had once been a prisoner of the Apache, but it was true. "They wanted to see if I would cry," she said, "but I did not."

Reuben asked if it wasn't true that if you did cry out they killed you, but if you kept silent they just kept up the torture until you called out or died anyway. Spring said it hadn't been true in her case or she wouldn't be alive. "I think they only test the men."

They finished their whispered discussion only to find Helen alert and wakeful and wanting to know more. She seemed to Reuben to be too interested in the details of the Apache tortures. As if she were planning to be a spectator rather than a participant.

When they left Sojurn, Reuben had only the most vague of plans: get away from the attack, get the girls to a place of safety. But now his lack of planning had caught up with them. They were not safe where they were. They would not be safe if they went forward. Unless...

"What if we were to join up with a California bound wagon train? We'd have the protection of being part of a larger group."

"California!" Helen protested.

"Oh yes, California. We can seek our fortune," Spring said.

It took several days of discussion—Helen, after all, had been promised St Louis, before they settled on California as their destination. The hard part lay in explaining to Helen that it was not quite as easy to find a wagon train returning to St Louis as it would be to flag down an east-bound trolley car on the streets of Philadelphia. "The wagon trains just go the one way, dear," Spring said, "They don't make return trips. In fact, they can't. When they get to California, they use the lumber in the wagons to build their houses. Nothing is left but the wheels."

"So there is no way to get home," Helen said mournfully, though of what home she could be thinking with her father dead, and her mother and younger brother still held captive by the Indians, Reuben and Spring Morning had no idea.

"Well, I suppose there are boats from San Francisco."

"We'll be together," Reuben ventured.

"We'll be together, I'm glad," said Helen and that decided it.

Gradually, they moved to a lower elevation. But, like it or not, the closer they came to the route of the wagon trains, the deeper they moved into Apache territory.

It had been Reuben's plan originally to head to the southwest, spending as little time as possible among the Apache. But regardless of his plans, the path they traveled always seemed to head southeast or even east by south for the southern and western routes all seemed to end in a sheer drop to the desert below.

It grew less humid as they descended and much hotter. They began to miss the dampness of the forest, though now they felt it had been the dampness that triggered Helen's fever.

Finding an evening resting place became more and more of a problem. Their camp had to be secluded, a place they could watch from without being watched in turn, for fear of the Apache. And it had to be near a source of water, a spring or a creek.

More and more, water had become the focus of their thoughts. If they could find water, they would probably be able to find edible plants and small animals near by. It would be cooler near the water.

Helen's thoughts were elsewhere. "Are there wolves where we are going?" Helen asked him one day, out of the blue. Apparently, she had read about wolves somewhere, perhaps in a story that someone had read to her.

"I don't think so," said Reuben, "But I don't know, I've never been this far West." It is to Reuben's credit that never once did it occur to him to lie to curry the young girl's favor. He was what he was and he did not dissemble, the product of his Quaker upbringing.

On their third day of scrambling down the uneven trail, sometimes riding, but more often leading the horses, they found themselves again walking along a cliff on the rim of the valley. To their north was a narrow opening, lush and green, with brambles across it. Below them, to the south, for as far as the eye could travel, stretched the desert. The empty land was devoid of trees; only a few low shrubs were to be found scattered irregularly along what might have been creek beds but were now only dry washes. Giant Saguaro cactus grew in clumps. One could almost reach out and touch them as if they were green dots on an oil painting.

"Is that a wagon trail?" Spring asked.

Reuben studied the faint lines to which Spring was pointing, from where the lines began in the sun's glare to the east to where they ended behind a rise in the west. Ruts left by wagon wheels? Perhaps. He could make out the remains of what might have been half a dozen campgrounds along the trail. And midway, below and to the east, wasn't that a wagon or the remains of one?

"I think it is," said Reuben. "I'd have to ride down and examine the marks to be sure. If it is, we can wait here and join up with the next train." If the wagons still use this route, he thought. If we can find some kind of creek that still has water that will keep us alive till the wagons come. And if the Apache don't find us first.

"They're a lot of if's," Spring said as if reading his mind.

"Are these safe to eat?" Helen asked. She had gathered a handful of plump green-purple berries and, humbled by her previous bad experiences, had brought them to Reuben to judge. He thought he had seen something like them before. "Gooseberries," he pronounced, sampling three or four of the ones she had given him.

The berries were a pleasant surprise. And where were berries, there was bound to be water somewhere nearby. Reuben dismounted and joined the girls in picking and eating as many of the berries as he could.

When they followed the berry bushes back into what they'd thought was only a cleft in the rock, they discovered the hidden canyon. At first glance, it seemed no more than fifteen or twenty yards in depth, but as they pushed their way deeper inside, they found a gently sloping terrace that extended more than fifty yards to the north.

Encircled by the canyon walls, the ground was folded in two from east to west so that it sloped in both directions concealing the rear of the canyon from the front. Forcing their way through the tall grass, they climbed up and over the low ridge. A waterfall tumbled down the cliff at the rear of the canyon; water from the previous night's storm still dripped from it into a large pool of clear water at its base.

"Water," said Spring, "As much water as we need."

"Look," said Helen, "Water." In a moment, she and Spring had taken off their moccasins and were wading giddily though the pool.

"You know," said Spring, "the water here is almost deep enough to bathe. If you would excuse us," she said to Reuben when he did not take the immediate hint.

Embarrassed, he headed back to the bluff to take a second look at the wagon trail. A family of jackrabbits scattered in every direction as he passed.

The horses had already found their way into the hidden canyon and were munching contentedly. Reuben knelt on the cliff's edge and looked down again into the valley below. "You know, I believe we could get from here to California," he said to no one in particular.

When he returned, the girls were standing giggling by the poolside. They had already laid out the bedrolls and unpacked the saddlebags, and were now examining their remaining clothing to see what they could put on. "Something as clean as we are," said Helen. She had found a skirt and blouse she'd been given back in Sojurn. The blouse was a tan color, the skirt a dark brown, and the colors set off Helen's own light complexion. Of an instant, Reuben felt that same rush of excitement he'd felt the day he first saw Helen standing by the river in the canyon. "Isn't it beautiful?" she asked, meaning her new clothes.

"Very, very beautiful," he replied, meaning the young woman inside them.

Spring had also been dressing in new clothes, a long gown ornamented with green and blue thread that Mrs. Flemming had discarded as "not her color." Spring wore the gown for only a few moments and then, motioning to Reuben to look away, began to take it off.

"But why are you taking off your dress?" cried Helen. "It's lovely."

"I don't want to ruin it," said Spring. "I'm sure to get grass stains."

"Who cares? It's beautiful."

"It is beautiful," Spring said softly, "I don't suppose it really matters." She put the dress on a second time. The dress was very beautiful and very much Spring's color.

"It's very attractive," Reuben said. "You are very beautiful, also," he added. Spring had neither expected nor asked for the compliment. She blushed. With her dark skin, now thoroughly tanned by the sun, the blush only made her look more attractive. "Thank you," she said.

They remained in the glade for four days, unable to decide whether to go forward or to stay there and wait for a wagon train. Each morning when they arose, one or the other of them would slip out to the mouth of the canyon and look down into the valley. Always the trail remained empty. No sign of a wagon train, no sign of a rider, single or in company, no sign of the Apache. They would inspect again at noon, at one, and perhaps at three. They would gaze out again across the valley for a short time before the evening meal and for a long time after as the sun set slowly and the west end of the valley glowed with fire. The wagon route from Tucson to California remained as before, tempting and empty.

We can go it alone, Reuben would say to himself, as another day passed without sign of movement on the trail. But he knew why the settlers traveled together in a train. Apache. Alone, the three of them might escape the notice of the Indians. But they could not begin to fight off an attack. Their only safety lay in traveling with a group of other white men headed for the west.

Meanwhile, they waited in the glade, feasting on the berries at the mouth of the canyon, catching and eating rabbits and woodchucks, and, once, a hawk that Spring brought down with a bowshot to the applause of two admiring onlookers.

Several large fish could be glimpsed hiding in the shallow pool beneath the waterfall and every morning, Reuben would toss out his line, baiting it with a stick-like insect, and soon reel in their breakfast. "Will we run out of fish?" Spring asked. "Maybe. Or maybe the ones that are left will just get fatter."

Despite their apparent happiness, they remained alert and watchful, whether it was day or night, on the lookout for signs of the hidden Apache camp. When they finally got to see an Apache and a wagon train, it was on the same day and at practically the same moment.

They were almost at the end of another day of indecisive idleness. Reuben and Spring were sitting discussing San Francisco. Helen was off by herself, sulking. As usual, once a plan was complete, she wanted the results now, and was unwilling to contemplate much less confront the consequences.

She had even announced she would go off alone on her pony if she had to wait much longer, and had begin packing her saddlebags with that end in mind. "Catch me a rabbit," she said to Reuben, "I'll need food on the trail."

"You'll need more than one rabbit to get you to California," he replied. Nonetheless, he and Spring had begun to realize that if they were going to get to California, it might well have to be on their own. Pleasant as it was, they could not stay forever in that glade.

The buck, a six-pronged antelope, ran by them and down the hillside, sprinting as if he'd already seen the arrow with his name on it. Equally quickly, acting with a reflex he'd not known he possessed, Reuben had the rifle to his shoulder cocked, aimed and ready to fire. Only the steady pressure of a hand on the barrel kept him from firing. He looked up; Spring was beside him, finger to lips: "Wait," she whispered. Across the glade, Helen was equally still; she sat kneeling, hands forward, like a woodchuck that has spotted danger.

The antelope leaped to the left, pulled back just as he would surely have gone over the cliff, made a final leap to the right that was almost a somersault, and fell dead, an arrow through his chest.

In an instant, they saw the Apache warrior sitting astride his deer. No sound had preceded his arrival, and almost no motion, nothing that would have given the hunter's presence away. In a short while, he was joined by two other hunters emerging from either side of the entrance to the small canyon that housed the fugitives' living quarters.

One of the new arrivals carried the dried, hollowed out head of a two-pronged antelope under his arm. You could see how the hunt had started: the real antelope walking along the path, stopping when he saw the second false antelope grazing quietly in the field. He goes up to him, perhaps nuzzling the second antelope nose to nose. He catches a false scent; he knows something is wrong; he runs and is brought down by the second hunter's arrow.

The decoy wore a buckskin vest over fringed breeches. A knife sheath and a long wooden tube were stuck through the rawhide belt around his waist. The brave's legs were bare, though long moccasins with turned-up soles protected his feet and ankles from the tough grass. Each of the braves carried a long knife in a sheath of buckskin hung from a rawhide belt. Quickly, the hunters put down their arrows, took out their knives, and set to work. They had gutted and skinned the deer almost before the life had left the animal's body.

Reuben sat motionless. Why haven't they seen us, Reuben thought, they've got to see us soon. He wanted to scrunch down flat against the ground, to become invisible, but he stayed unmoving, knowing that their only safety lay in being another leaf on the tree, another inanimate part of the land around them.

He had the rifle of course. It was part of him now, part of his frozen extended arm. The night before, planning to go hunting, he'd rubbed the rifle barrel with soot from the fire, so that the reflection of the sun on the barrel would not give his presence away.

With no more than three or four quick words exchanged, the hunters completed their task and still without noticing the presence of the three watchers, started off down the hillside. To Reuben's unbelieving eye, Spring followed them, moving as swiftly and as silently as the three Apache warriors.

For ten long agonizing minutes, Helen and Reuben sat unmoving, as still as they had been when the Apache were there. Then Spring returned. "Why so quiet?" she said, "the Indians are already back in their camp."

"Where is it?" Reuben asked. The tension in his voice only seemed to amuse Spring; "Just around the corner," she said; "Helen and I may go shopping there tomorrow for a new dress." She curtsied.

Reuben looked at her, glaring; then he burst into laughter. Spring laughed with him.

Strangely, Helen did not join in their laughter, but sat as stiff and rigid as when the Apache were near. "Look," Helen said and pointed. At the far eastern end of the great valley, where the last rays of the setting sun were still to be seen painting the hills, a faint cloud of dust could just be made out.

Chapter 15

"Seriously," Reuben asked Spring, "How far away is the Apache camp?"

"It's just two arroyos to the East. You take the path up instead of down. We're lucky we haven't seen them before this."

"There can't be too many of them."

"There's a lot, at least ten teepees and a wickiup, women and children as well as men."

"We should get out of here," said Reuben pacing restlessly.

"We've been safe so far."

"What about the wagon train?" Helen asked. "Are they safe?"

"Maybe the train is what the Apache have been waiting for," Spring volunteered; "they may plan on stealing the horses."

"And taking slaves," Helen said shivering.

Spring put an arm around her. "No," Spring lied, "They probably just want the horses." She hugged her young companion.

For a long while, no one said anything. Behind them, a rabbit triggered one of their snares. They could hear it struggling. "The Apache will attack just as the sun sets," Reuben said. "That way, they'll have the sun behind them as they approach the train. We'd better pack and get ready to follow them. If we stay close we'll be O.K."

"Follow them? Pack everything?" Helen cried.

"Pack everything," Reuben repeated. "We have to be ready to move on an instant's notice."

"We'll follow them as closely as we can. So the Apache will think the sounds and the dust of our horses are from their own party. They'll have the same problem the settlers will, picking us out against the setting sun.

"If they're beaten off by the settlers, and I hope they will be, then we'll join the wagon train. Otherwise, we'll just have to go off by ourselves."

"Oh those poor people; the children," Helen cried.

"The Apache are too close to where we are camped now," Reuben said, "and with so many of them, they are bound to find us sooner or later. While their attention is focused on the wagon train, may be our only chance to escape."

"I don't like leaving," Helen said to Spring and looked around at the narrow plateau that had been their home for so many days. Spring followed her gaze to the little grove of trees that hid the fishing and washing pool, the line of berry bushes that still bore the last of the late fall crop, the tall grass that hid the deer mice and the two families of rabbits. "I know what you mean," she said and stroked the younger girl's hair.

For almost an hour, as the sun sank ever lower in the sky, the three stood motionless on the ledge where the Apache hunters had perched only a short while before. Their horses, already burdened with their packs and fresh water, stirred restlessly beside them.

While they watched, the wagon train came to a halt. The cloud of dust that had surrounded the train disappeared slowly in the wind rising from the valley. One could imagine the men getting down from the wagons to stretch their legs, the women reaching back to pull out the cooking utensils.

Little dots of flame rose from around the camped train as the settlers made cooking fires to prepare their evening meal. Each fire yielded a slender plume of smoke that told a story to the watchers.

"Don't they know the cooking fires give their position away, let all their enemies know there's a wagon train camped there?" said Helen breathlessly. You could tell she had gone back into her childhood and was thinking of the wagon train her family had belonged to.

Spring answered, "Maybe they already know they have been seen, dear, and their fires are to send out a message, 'Attack us if you dare. We have many guns, many brave warriors.'"

"Let's hope the wagon train has the firepower to deliver on its threat." But Reuben's voice held no promise of success.

The sun sank lower, quickly, so that soon only the tips of the surrounding peaks would be on fire. Across the valley and on about the same level, though to the East of their own position, a tall column of smoke appeared. The column broke into puffs, reformed and broke again.

"More Apache," Reuben said, "They are signaling to the ones over here."

"What if one of the Apache sees us?" Helen asked.

"They're concentrating on the train below," Reuben replied. "If we stay close enough, they'll think we're part of their raiding party. We'll follow them and turn off just before they get to the wagon train."

"Should work," said Spring showing her teeth in a smile.

"Maybe," Reuben said and smiled back. He reached out, touched her fingers and began to laugh. Soon they were both laughing.

"What are you laughing about?" said Helen.

"It's better than crying," sang Spring and laughed again.

Suddenly, they heard the sound of hoof beats and their laughter faded abruptly. Below and to their left, rider after rider appeared on the slope heading for the valley beneath. Each rider wore painted markings on his face. Each had a bow slung over his shoulder, though one or two also carried rifles. Some carried bags of pitch and tar in back of their saddles. "For the fire arrows," Spring said.

Nine, ten,..., nineteen Indians went down the mountain ten to twenty seconds apart.

"Mount your horses," Reuben said. Twenty more seconds passed but no more Indians appeared. The interval stretched to thirty seconds than forty. After a full minute had passed, Reuben gave a quick hand signal, "Go."

Reuben carried the carbine ready in his fingers, reins firmly in the other hand. Helen and Spring followed, each with a six-shooter on their saddle nearby. The horses—Champion, the Pinto, and the big Bay, went slip, sliding down the steep slope.

The ground was crisscrossed with rivulets and small channels worn by the rain. Occasionally, a clump of earth would break off after the horses passed and roll down the mountain.

In the gathering dusk, Reuben had no choice but to follow the Apache closely. When the last of the riders cut left, Reuben watched and waited and then cut left in his turn. One of the Indians would look back and see them; they would have to take their chances. There was an even bigger risk that one or the other of their own horses would stumble and pitch them down the slope. Despite or because of the danger, Reuben plunged on at breakneck speed.

Tufts of grass and sagebrush flew between the horses' hooves along with dried up petals from the small red flowers that covered the dry slope, a whole fragrant field of flowers which joined with the fierce smell of horses and riders. Below them, just barely outlined by the setting sun, the smoke of cooking fires rose from the halted wagon train. Across the valley, invisible, charged the second band of Indians.

The ground was almost level as they reached the floor of the valley proper. Reuben could see the ruts left by the wheels of previous wagon trains, the signs of campfires and many horses. A roadrunner, disturbed by their movement, crossed the path in front of them, beak, long neck, and legs a single line.

With the sun down and the moon hours from rising, Reuben could barely discern the silhouette of the rider ahead of him. Then, abruptly, the silhouette disappeared. The rider had toppled from his horse. He could be seen running forward until he caught up with the next rider and leapt up bareback behind him. The injured animal, ankle broken, rocking back and forth in pain, was abandoned on the ground.

Why am I doing this, Reuben asked himself, at the same time as he urged his own steed onwards. Behind him, Helen and Spring, still trusting in Reuben's judgment, continued to race pell-mell down the slope.

A shot rang out from the direction of the wagon train, then another and another. The air was filled with the war whoops of the Apache. The first of the fire arrows soared through the air to be followed by a second and a third. A wagon burst into flame and the settlers near it became easy targets for the Indians.

The orange and yellow glow spread as a second wagon was set on fire. Reuben could hear the men calling to one another, arranging too late for mutual aid, just as the settlers had waited till too late at Sojurn. Something broke inside of him. They're all dead, he mourned, thinking of Mike Forester and the others they had left behind at Sojurn. He turned Champion and started off at right angles to the path of the wagon train. "To the South," he pointed, motioning for Spring and Helen to bring their horses close to him, "we'll wait there."

They followed, relying more on his gestures for guidance than on the words that were lost in the wind of their passage. "I don't think many from the train will survive," said Spring when they had pulled up for a moment on the far hillside. "Perhaps we should go south after all, to Mexico. As soon as the Apache have left."

"We'll wait," Reuben said. He was again firmly in command of himself.

"Till they leave?"

"Till just before dawn. Then, we'll go down to the wagon train and see if we can help any who've survived."

Chapter 16

About an hour after moonrise, the Apache war party withdrew. A few led strings of horses, along with several larger animals that might have been oxen. Others had small figures sitting before them on the saddle. All dragged sacks of booty behind their horses.

The war party had passed quickly through the desecrated train. Apparently, their chief interest was in rifles and horses, though Reuben had seen one warrior outlined in the firelight with a woman's dress thrown over his arm. Occasionally, the watchers on the hillside would hear screams, long piercing cries that would end abruptly in a whimper. More fires broke out as the Apache fired the few remaining intact wagons.

Reuben gave the Apache no more than ten or fifteen minutes to disappear in the darkness to the North before signaling the two girls to remount and follow him down the slope.

During the night, Spring and Helen had lain close together with Reuben near by. Helen had slept, but quiet though Spring appeared to be, Reuben knew she too was listening, hearing the echoes of those screams behind her closed eyelids.

The wagon train glowed dully, like the remnants of a hundred campfires. Everything had been put to the torch; here and there a wagon canopy could be seen with a scrap of fabric still adhering to it, but most were bare skeletons.

Reuben thought immediately of Sojurn, of the burned out houses, and of the dead and the dying they had left behind on their flight.

A charred corpse swung to and fro suspended by one leg from a wagon canopy. Under the head was a pile of charred lumber ripped from the wagon. The wood had been piled beneath the still-living victim and then set afire. The skull had exploded from the heat and now the corpse's face was alien and unrecognizable.

Other corpses hung from the surrounding wagons. Sometimes a man and a woman would be hanging side by side, the woman's body slightly smaller, slightly shorter than the man's.

The lucky ones—a child's body pierced by an arrow, a man with his throat cut, lay on the ground. Many of the settlers had been trapped, burned alive within their wagons. They could see few signs of an organized resistance, except at the far end of the wagon train where some of the wagons had been drawn into a circle. Most of the settlers appeared to have been lying inside their wagons, sick from dysentery, perhaps, when the raid began.

"There weren't enough who weren't sick to drive the Indians away," whispered Spring.

"Where are the children?" he whispered back.

"Children?" she echoed pointing with horror to a child's body suspended in the air, the spear that had taken the child's life fixing it forever to the ground.

"There aren't enough bodies here," he said; "these are large wagons, built to hold entire families. The Apache have taken the children to raise as their own. Like you and Helen."

"Raise them or sell them as slaves," Spring whispered.

Corpses lay everywhere. Women and babies with arrows through them, men who had died with their guns in their hands. More corpses could be found, charred beyond recognition of any humanity. They found a man alive beneath one of the wagons. "Kill me," he said. Reuben studied the man's wounds, knife thrusts designed not to kill but to cause unending pain. He brought out his gun and placed it against the man's temple.

"Wait," said Spring and put her hand on Reuben's arm.

He waited, his gun cocked, while the man whimpered that he wanted to die. "I hear voices." Spring said. Soon Reuben could hear them, too. Men's voices, five or six different men. They were not speaking English.

Reuben could see Helen across the way, her body pressed against a burned-out wagon, frozen and unmoving. Apparently, Helen could see what they could only hear.

A single voice cut through the night followed by a burst of laughter. How could someone laugh at a scene like this? "What language is that?" Reuben asked.

"The men are speaking Spanish," Spring said. "They say the Indians are fools to leave so much behind. Apparently, they found gold in one of the wagons. And they are taking the jewelry from the dead people's fingers."

Bringing life to Spring's words, a bandit appeared in Reuben's line of sight; the man bent over a body on the ground and began to pry off the wedding ring. When the ring would not come off readily, the bandit opened a clasp knife and hacked the finger off. Spring gasped. The bandit held out the finger for all his companions to see, then tossed both ring and finger into a pouch at his belt.

"If the bandits come back here, we'll kill as many as we can," Reuben said. Spring nodded, but Reuben could see she was visibly shaken and would probably be of no use this time if it came to a gunfight.

The bandits, there were two of them, continued to move down the line of wagons toward where Reuben and the girls were hiding. They were no more than twenty feet from Reuben and Spring, when a six-gun went off in the air, once, twice.

"Banditos," came the cry. At the far end of the encampment, in the circle where the settlers had tried to build their last stand against the Indians, stood an imposing figure clearly illuminated in the light from the many remaining fires. A man much taller than the others, he wore a low-crowned broad-brimmed vicuna hat with a gilt band around its crown. His short jacket with roll collar and wide lapels bore two rows of bright gold buttons. The sash at his waist was of bright gold. And his tall black leather boots were ornamented with bright gold stitching. "Banditos," he repeated in a low penetrating voice.

It was his solidly built companion, a stocky half-breed Mexican, who had fired the six-gun into the air. The man, himself, carried a rifle swinging freely in one hand and Reuben knew, somehow, the bandit would not hesitate to use it.

"He could be my father," Spring said, hypnotized. Helen was riveted, also, eyes wide and staring, fixed upon the man.

The bandits near them had turned at the sound of their chief's voice and were walking quickly back to where he stood. Reuben breathed a sigh of relief as they left. They were safe then, though the bandits could return at any moment. Reuben used this opportunity to slip over to Helen's side and throw an arm about her shoulders. Spring followed quickly after him.

Helen was holding a lace handkerchief all twisted between her fingers. "Where did you get the handkerchief?" Spring asked. The girl did not answer; her eyes were riveted upon the bandit chief. "Helen, you took that handkerchief from one of the wagons didn't you?" Spring chastised. "It's so pretty," Helen said.

From their new position, they could see more clearly into the space where the bandits had gathered. The bandit chief was holding up the loot, like trophies, for the other bandits to see and applaud. From time to time, he would summon one of the other bandits to him and give him a hug. The gold and jewelry were the common share; clothing, women's dresses and blankets that the Indians had overlooked became the individual property of the bandit who was despicable enough to remove them from the slain.

The bandit chief spoke to his men at length and Spring translated what she could hear above the sound of men's voices going "Ole" and "Oja" as each new piece of stolen property was revealed. The chief spoke, often, of his men's brave deeds, though what had they done, Reuben thought, but to wait, cowering in fear of the Apache, until all danger was past and then to rob the dead.

Suddenly the bandit chief stopped his peroration and looked straight toward them. Through a trick of the firelight, his pale face and deep-set dark eyes seemed to loom in the air before them as if he were only a few feet away.

"He sees me," Helen cried and shrank back into Reuben's arms.

Indeed, the bandit chief was now walking toward them as if he had uncovered their hiding place; his every step brought them closer and closer to exposure.

Helen whimpered. "It's all right," Spring whispered trying to calm her, "he can't have seen us."

Midway across the square, the bandit chief stopped and gestured to his men. From out of the shadow of the wagons, three men were dragged forward, settlers who somehow, miraculously, had survived the Apache attack. Two of the men were hurt; one dragged a leg behind him. The bandits who pulled the three forward into the firelight paid no attention to the men's injuries but jerked them upright in the presence of the bandit chief.

"He is asking them if there is more gold," Spring translated. Not satisfied with the response, the bandit chief signaled that one of the men should be thrust forward. The bandit chief reached out, one long arm extended, and cupped the man's jaw brutally in his hand.

The man struggled, his face contorted, and tried to free himself. The bandit chief increased the pressure until the man had no choice but to look upward into the bandit chief's eyes. The man spat straight into the bandit chief's face. Good for you, Reuben thought.

A sharp crack sounded through the encampment as the bandit backhanded the man across the face. Spring and Helen recoiled at the sound. The man's jaw hung limply, broken from the single slap; he wobbled and remained upright only because the bandits held him. Helen whimpered a second time.

The bandit chief stepped back. At a signal from him, the bandits released the three men and formed into a circle around them. The man who had been punished sank slowly to his knees. The bandit chief's sidekick grunted his displeasure and motioned to the remaining two settlers to hold up their companion. They hastened to lift him to an upright position, though his head lolling limply against his breastbone signaled he was still unconscious. The bandit chief raised his rifle, still holding it loosely in one hand, and pointed it at the unconscious man's legs. Tightening his grasp on the handle, he fired once, twice. The other bandits fired their pistols also. The men inside the circle danced with the pain of the bullets, skipping from leg to leg trying to avoid injury. The unconscious man slipped from their support and was soon lying bullet-ridden on the ground. The bandit chief raised his rifle a second time. Soon one of the two remaining victims had taken a bullet in the leg and was lying on the ground beside the first. The third settler lasted longer and died more painfully, from a shot in his spine.

As the sound of the gunshots died away, the bandits dashed for their horses. "They are afraid the Apache will return," Spring said. Then the bandits were gone. "We must go too," said Reuben. "Leave the handkerchief," he said to Helen. "But it's so pretty," she repeated, though by now the handkerchief was all black and sooty from her hands. "Leave it," he commanded.

They headed South, away from the wagon train, away from the Apache, away, they hoped, toward Mexico.

Chapter 17

Another day of riding brought them to a small town that had grown up by the side of a narrow riverbed. The town held a mercantile and a cantina, a church and a hostler with a smithy at its side.

The river made its way to the town through a series of small canyons, deep gorges in some cases, wide alluvial plains in others. In the flattened areas where the river overflowed its banks, long narrow strips of cultivated fields served like signboards to announce the town's presence long before they got there.

Here, as in Sojurn, the people seemed very friendly. But the three were more reluctant now to make friends of people who might soon perish.

The day was a Sunday and they could hear church bells ringing. "I want to go to church," Helen said. Reuben knew something of churches, though it was a long time since he had seen the inside of one, and he said sure, he would go along.

Thirty or forty people were crowded into a small one-room building. A weird mixture of the old and childless young, mostly white but some Mexican. The parishioners did not stare at them as they walked in the door, though they must have known the three were strangers, but only smiled at them briefly as if to indicate they were glad Reuben and his two companions had joined them. Still, the three were conscious throughout the service of one or more pairs of eyes constantly upon them. One little girl in the front row turned full around to stare at them until pushed down firmly in her seat by her father.

The church was Protestant of a denomination Reuben had never heard of though the service seemed familiar enough to Helen. The preacher, a tall, cadaverous man with hollow cheeks and long sideburns, spoke out against Popishness, (a poor choice of topic Reuben thought with Spring and so many other obvious Catholics in the room), and of the ungodliness of holy water, incense, candles and other popish deviltry. In fact, Reuben thought, the sermon dealt altogether too much with what shouldn't be than with what should.

After the sermon, the parishioners made much of the two girls. Offers were made of food and lodging, even of clothes if the weary travelers needed them. The food they accepted. They—Spring—turned down the lodging and said they would camp out by the canyon where they'd spent the night before. Helen looked as if she might have preferred to spend the night in a feather bed in town but didn't offer any protest. Helen seemed much quieter now than she had before her sickness, quieter and more reflective.

Reuben, too, was noticed in passing. After the invariable question, "And how did you like the sermon?" he was told plenty of good farmland was still available in the area, that is, if he wasn't afraid of hard work. From the glances he and his clothing received, he got the impression that many of the townsfolk thought he might be. Maybe he looked too elegant, too much the dude. He'd dressed that morning in his best buckskin-fringed riding pants and he'd brushed off and worn his finest Stetson. So the people of Hostler's Rest didn't think he could do a good day's work. Well, that was their problem.

"What did you think of that sermon?" Reuben asked Spring, when they had returned to the gorge to camp for the night.

"Did you see their clothes?" Helen interrupted, "All the women here seem to have beautiful clothes, much prettier than in Sojurn."

"They're a lot like the folks in Sojurn aren't they," said Spring.

"Why do you say that?"

"Oh, Abe Simpson is sort of like Mike Forester. You notice how everyone seems to rely on his opinion. The Thompsons are like the Stewarts."

"Two or three of the men could be another Micah," Reuben said, though he wasn't sure he wanted to play the game. He'd liked the people he'd met in Sojurn very much and he wasn't yet willing to surrender old friends for new.

"There's no one quite like Pegleg," said Helen joining in. Pegleg, a nonstop talker they'd met at the potluck that afternoon, ran the general store. "What about Clem, the prospector?" replied Spring, "He was a character, too."

"I wonder if Clem got away?" Helen asked innocently.

Clem didn't, thought Reuben, no one got away from Sojurn. Only the three of us.

"This food is good," said Spring changing the subject. Single-handed, she had put away almost a full rack of ribs. "They've even got pigs here. Pigs, chickens, cows."

"And pastry," said Helen smacking her lips.

"Those honey tarts were made by that widow woman, Mrs. T."

"Who looks just like Mrs. F."

"Exactly," said Spring.

"Do you think she'll go all gooey over Reuben, too?"

"You don't know what you are talking about," Reuben said. "Stop it."

"All goo-goo eyes and it's so nice to have a man around the house."

"Oh Reuben." cried Spring pretending to faint.

"Stop that!" Reuben demanded a second time. But the more he protested, the more the girls laughed and made fun of him. He walked away from them finally, though not forgetting to take some ribs and a slice of homemade pie on the walk with him.

After supper, while Helen lay down by the fire, saying she was tired and wanted to sleep, Spring walked out to where Reuben was sulking. "I like the people here," said Spring, "I know you're reluctant to like anyone after Sojurn, but these seem to be good people."

"What about that crazy minister?" said Reuben, "He seemed to preach a lot of hate for a man whose God preaches love."

"He's just one person Reuben. They're not all like that."

Yes they are, thought Reuben. I had a friend in Sojurn and he's dead. If I make a friend here, he'll die too.

Spring put her hand in his. He tried to draw his hand away but she would not let him. She said, "The Indians of the Canyon think the spirits of the dead are always with us. They eat, they hunt, they ride with us along the river. When you die you just go on to another phase of life."

"It's not the dying," Reuben said. "The Apache didn't just kill all those innocent people in the wagon train, they tortured them first; they took their scalps and skinned them while they were still living. They took their blankets and their horses. Then the bandits came and took what was left." Reuben hadn't been able to put all his feelings into words; Spring could sense an unasked question, "Am I like that? Like the Apache, like the bandits, cruel and uncaring?"

"People can also do good," Spring said. "They can deal honestly with one another, protect the weak, and share with their neighbors. I think you're like that, Reuben."

"All the good people I know are dead. And we don't really know these new people," Reuben gasped.

"Well, you know yourself. And nothing prevents you from doing good while you can, Reuben Lee, nothing but a lot of self-pity." She released his fingers just at the moment he would like to have held hers tighter, and walked away from him.

Reuben walked in the opposite direction, away from the camp, to where the canyon lay sleeping in the moonlight. The land below was flat and regular. In some places, the river was almost flush with its banks. Surely in Spring, it must actually flood the land around it. The line of trees and shrubs along the riverbank could be removed and the rest of the land put into cultivation as the other farmers had done.

The other farmers said they got two, sometimes three crops a year—maize, beans, squash, melons, lettuce. He could see the growth in the valley bottom was rich and luxuriant. Some of the settlers had experimented with barley. Reuben wondered, given the amount of water available, if it might not be possible to plant cotton.

"Am I a farmer?" Reuben asked himself. My father was a farmer and his father and his father's father before him. My family owned five thousand acres of prime river bottom. My family owns them still, though they are divided now among four squabbling brothers and sisters. I can do better than they can, he thought.

When he returned to the camp, both the girls were fast asleep. He moved his bedroll closer to theirs, placed his arm over his eyes to shield them from the moon and was soon fast asleep as well.

Reuben and Spring had more or less the same conversation the next day after Reuben had returned from town.

The girls had chosen to stay out by the river where they were camped and wash their clothes. "Got some more food," he said when he came back. "More food and more invitations. These people are nice.

"They say if we were to settle on the land, we could get the seed and the tools on credit. That's what they say."

"Oh Reuben, that's wonderful," Spring said. She waited for him to continue and tried to look encouraging. She could tell he was both excited at the prospect of settling down yet fighting with himself at the same time against the idea.

"Don't get too enthusiastic. That's just what they say. But the fellow I spoke to, Rand something, didn't seem to know how much they charge in interest. If they charge too much, all you're doing is 'cropping. No point in 'cropping. You're always trying to catch up. You never get to own your own land."

"But you don't know what the interest rate is yet, do you?" Spring said to him later that evening after Helen had gone to bed, again much earlier than she and Reuben would have expected. "You don't know if it's going to be high or if it's going to be low, yet you're sitting there stewing about it, thinking people are going to cheat you."

"I haven't made up my mind about settling down here yet. I'm thinking about it." He paused. "To tell you the truth, Spring, I haven't had much luck with people."

"Reuben you don't know people. You know fantasies. Sometimes I think you just live in your head. You make up stories about the people you meet, long before you get to know them properly; then, you go ahead and act as if your fantasy is the real person. If it is, then fine. If it isn't, you feel that person cheated you in some way."

"Huh," is what Reuben said in reply and then he and Spring sat in silence until all light had vanished from the sky and they had no alternative but to go to sleep.

"The credit is real after all," Reuben announced a day later.

Helen was laying out all her clothes again for the third time that day, while Spring was preparing a meal from a mixture of what they had been given the day before, cooked food and fresh vegetables.

"See," Spring said, "I told you: you have to trust people."

"Abe says all the land to the West of town is taken. But we could farm here, for example, where we are now. I kind of like this place."

"I do too," said Spring.

"It's quiet and it kind of reminds me..."

"Of the Canyon," she finished his sentence.

"Did you like it there at all, Spring? In the Canyon?"

"Sometimes," she said. "And sometimes I didn't like it all."

They stopped talking and stood silent, side by side. Reuben pointed into the canyon. "You notice it's all flat down there. Water doesn't seem to be moving too fast. That land on the edge where all the cattails are growing. I bet you could grow cotton. I wonder if anyone has ever grown cotton around here. If you got cotton, then you can put up a mill, make your own clothes.

"That reminds me. They say you and Helen can get clothes in the mercantile in town. Any kind of clothes you want. On credit. Pay them back when our crop comes in."

"What about St Louis?"

"I've thought about that. You know those eastern cities are pretty expensive. I thought if we could stay here for awhile, make some money farming, then Helen and I could go back to the city."

"I think Helen would like that. Staying here for a while, I mean. I think she want to stay in one place and not have to move around. Too much has happened. She may talk about going to St Louis, but I think what she really wants is a place where she can be sure of sleeping in the same bed every night. You've seen how she fusses over her pony and her clothes. Checks her bedroll half a dozen times each day to be sure that everything is where it should be. You notice that we've stayed out here and haven't gone into town. I mean, I'd like to go in town; I'd like some new clothes. But Helen keeps saying, 'tomorrow, tomorrow,' and we never go. She fusses sometimes if I go away without telling her, even if I only walk down to the river. She worries too, Reuben, when you're not here."

"See. It's all settled then," said Reuben obtusely. "We'll stay here and farm for awhile. I wonder if you can grow cotton. I wonder if anyone has tried.

"They say we have neighbors in that direction." He jerked his thumb toward the southeast along the river. "Their name is Crockett. I wonder if Mr. Crockett has tried to grow cotton. Say, you want to ride down to his place with me and find out?"

"I think I'd better stay with Helen."

"As you wish," Reuben said. "I'll be back by supper time. We'll cook that corn."

The Crockett's were a slightly older version of the family Reuben had stayed with briefly in Sojurn. She was a china doll of a woman, complete with red markings on each cheek; he was a beefy red-faced man who walked with a slight stoop, probably as a result of constantly bending over to talk with his china-doll wife.

Mr. Crockett thought it might be possible to grow cotton. Certainly, he'd had great luck with everything he'd tried. "Why I can grow enough melons here for the entire valley." Of course, that was the problem. All the farmers could. And while they could count on bountiful crops, they had no way yet to turn the crop into cash. "There'll be a railroad here someday," said Mr. Crockett, but Reuben could tell he was already slightly discouraged. Reuben was a little discouraged, also. Without a cash crop, how could he pay back his loan, how would he be able to buy all the little things Helen and he would need around the house? For that matter, how had the Crocketts' acquired so many possessions? "Sometimes, we sell food to the army," Mr. Crockett said.

The Crockett's house looked as if it had been transplanted in its entirety from the banks of the Ohio. Small knick-knacks were displayed on the hand-made furniture—a hutch and a china cabinet, which Reuben thought most settlers would have had to do without.

He thanked Mr. Crockett as they walked out together to inspect a field the elderly farmer was trying with barley; a line of bright green along one side was given over to beans. Then, he stepped back inside the house again to thank Mrs. Crockett for her hospitality.

A beautiful white blanket was spread over a chair in the parlor. A line of identical blue horses pulled identical blue buggies along its border. Mrs. Crockett was scraping at one corner of the blanket, trying to remove what seemed to be a soot stain. When she noticed Reuben's eyes on the blanket, she said defensively, "Just a small stain. It's a beautiful blanket, really. Bill brought it back from the mercantile today."

Reuben said nothing. He looked again at the pattern: Blue horses with a blue gentleman in a blue buggy behind them, lifting his whip.

"You look pale. Is anything wrong, Mr. Lee?"

"I thought I'd seen another blanket like it," Reuben said.

"Well, they say this design is all the style back East," Mr. Crockett replied with forced heartiness.

The awkward silence only grew deeper as each of the three sought for something reassuring to say.

"We thank you for coming Mr. Lee," Mrs. Crockett spoke finally, rescuing them.

"I thank you for your hospitality," Reuben replied. As if in a dream, he saw himself walk down off the porch and swing himself up into Champion's saddle. He waved. They waved back. The elderly couple remained on their front veranda waving as he rode back in the direction of his own farm-to-be.

He had seen the blue and white blanket before. Only a few days earlier. It had been wrapped around the legs of a dead woman. And then it had appeared in the hands of the bandit chief.

Chapter 18

Where the cross once made of silver,
now is caked with rust,
And the Sunday morning sermons pander to their lust,
Oh, the fallen face of Jesus is chokin' in the dust,
And Heaven only knows in which God they can trust.
   Phil Ochs

That morning, after tending to the horses, Reuben rode into town. His first stop was the general store.

Although he had been in the store briefly the previous day, he now looked around it as though for the first time. The store carried clothing—both men's and women's, farm tools, and seed too, of course. The men's clothing was the expected, bib overalls for working in the fields, work shirts and fancy, and boots—I should have a better pair of boots, Reuben thought, his own were scratched and abraded, the soles worn almost completely through; his moccasins too were unusable. A bin held carefully folded dress shirts cut in the Virginia style so that you didn't need to wear a collar with them. A couple of waist coats hung on wooden pegs, though he couldn't think of anybody other than the minister who was likely to be wearing one in town.

The woman's wear, some on racks, most in bins, was mostly petticoats and dresses with a few bonnets. Reuben couldn't help notice the luxurious quality of many of the items—French lace and fancy embroidery. The collection of farm tools was unusual, too. The store seemed to have one of every possible model. Reuben was used to a general store where you might find four identical scythes leaning back to back, not four scythes from four manufacturers.

Here, each fine-toothed rake was a different height and bore a different maker's brand. Made in New York, made in Pennsylvania.

He looked closely at one of the scythes. The initials J.H. were carved into its handle. "Some of this stuff is used," he said to the man behind the counter. Pegleg his name was or, rather, was what the folks in Hosteller's Rest called him because of the artificial leg he wore.

"Oh, aye. You know how it is. Farming is hard work. A lot of those who start out give up after a while. But if you're willing to work hard, you can make a go of it around here."

I've heard that before, Reuben thought. He was wearing his work clothes that morning, buckskin riding-chaps over a heavy cloth work pant. I'm willing to work hard, he thought.

"Where did they go?" he asked innocently.

"Who?" Pegleg said.

"The ones who didn't make it. J.H. here for instance."

"Ah, J.H. California mostly. Although some's headed back East."

"What was his name?" Reuben asked.

"Who?"

"J.H."

"Ah, J.H. Jim something. Jim Hancock." Pegleg's face reddened. He seemed to have swallowed his tongue.

"It doesn't matter," said Reuben. "What I did want to ask you is where I can take land. I mean what is available?"

"Generally a man can take what isn't claimed. You'd have to see Abe Simpson to get a map, but I think you'd be safe to set up your farm where you are now."

"You know where we're camped?" Reuben asked, incredulous.

"This is a small town, most folks know what's goin' on 'fore it's in the paper. But don't worry, we don't stick our noses in other people's business. Your wife now. A lot of men here took Mexican wives. You saw that in church."

"She's Spanish," Reuben corrected almost by reflex. "And she's not..." He stopped, realizing he was not quite sure himself what his relationship with Spring was.

"Spanish, French, Mexican, they're all the same. As long as they're good Protestants, they're welcome here in Hosteller's Camp and, confidentially..." The storekeeper motioned Reuben to come closer indicating he was about to speak in great confidence though his whisper was as clear and loud as his normal voice had been, "Many of the folks around here are Catholics. Your wife, too, I reckon. We don't care as long as they go to church.

"And what can I do for you Ms. Parks?" the storekeeper said, resuming his normal speaking voice; a tiny bell had already signaled the woman entrance into the store.

"My wife?" Reuben persisted, "You think Spring is my wife?"

"I imagine t'other, Helen, is your daughter, though she could be your sister. As I say, around here we don't poke our nose in t'others business." He turned his back on Reuben to wait on the new customer and Reuben was left to browse once more through the bin of men's shirts and the rack of women's dresses.

Not for one minute had Reuben believed the story Pegleg told him. Pegleg's red face, his stops and starts and hesitations had given the lies away. He didn't know who J.H. was, that was certain. Probably no one knew J.H., anymore. J.H. was dead, his body food for coyotes, somewhere on that same wagon trail where the other settlers had died. Maybe he'd been on the same train the three of them had witnessed the attack on. Maybe that was J.H.'s blanket in the Crockett's house, and J.H.'s wife's petticoats here in the bin before him.

How could this have happened, Reuben asked himself? How could people behave this way? Living like scavengers on the misery of others.

Abe Simpson had a farm just outside of the town. Abe, as Spring had recognized, was something like the mayor of the tiny village. Abe wasn't at his farm when Reuben got there, but Reuben tracked him down finally at the home of a neighbor who was kind enough to leave the room while Abe and Reuben talked. Abe heard Reuben out, but he had no sympathy for him. "Things you can't change it's best to live with," Abe said.

Reuben wanted to shout, "It's more than pretending ignorance, you're sharing in those bandits' spoils," but he choked back the words. He had a family to protect now. He left Abe dissatisfied and with only the most vague of promises they would talk about it some more.

"Spring! Helen! I've got something to tell you," Reuben said immediately when he got back to their camp.

"Us too," replied Helen.

"You've been to town," Reuben said flatly.

"Yes," Spring admitted crestfallen.

"We've got some wonderful new dresses," Helen said.

"You know where the dresses came from?" Reuben demanded.

"Yes, Reuben," Spring replied. "I saw one of the bandits, two actually. They were sitting drinking in the cantina that sits behind the general store. They were drinking and talking in Spanish."

"What were they talking about?" Reuben pressed on with his questions.

"Reuben, I don't want to answer. Helen liked the dress so much. You should have seen her face when she tried it on and she wanted so much to show the dress to you."

"It's beautiful," said Helen. "Let me put it on. Even if I may not be going to another dance for a long, long while."

"We've got to get away from here," Reuben said. He would not look at Helen.

"Where to? I think we are out of places to go," Spring replied. She was trying to sound reasonable but was under tension herself.

"Then we'll get the other settlers together and we'll drive the bandits away." Even as he spoke the words, Reuben it was an impossibility.

"I think maybe the people here do not want the bandits to go."

"The bandits here!" said Helen excitedly. Had she heard nothing else of what they were saying, Reuben thought angrily. Her face was flushed. She seemed not at all frightened, only intrigued at the prospect of seeing the bandit chief once more.

"I don't know what to do," he said that evening to Spring. As usual, after Helen had gone to bed, the two of them had gone for a short walk along the canyon's rim.

"Whatever you decide," she said.

"Well, I haven't decided anything," he stammered.

"I'll go along with it." When she saw this remark only made him more confused and angry, Spring added, "we'll work together, Reuben. We know we can count on each other."

"That's right," he said.

Chapter 19

Reuben woke to a morning of pink and gold, radiant beneath a cloudless sky. It promised to be another hot, scorching day, but he was no longer afraid of the heat, not while the river rolled by inexorably below him.

After breakfast, he rode into town in search of the man, Rand something, who'd first suggested they might stay and farm. When Reuben could not find Rand, he went on to the church to look for the minister, Mr. Faulkner. The church was locked, but he found the minister in back of the building raking in a garden that consisted mainly of thistles and yarrow. "The native flowers," Mr. Faulkner explained, "I like them the best. I've even had some of the vestrymen bring me some cactus."

"Mr. Faulkner..." Reuben began. He was not sure how to proceed.

"Reuben Lee, isn't it. Don't tell me, I remember. I'm so glad you dropped by. Will you and your family be settling in town then?"

"Can we leave?" challenged Reuben, "Can we leave really? Are we free to come and go, knowing what we do?"

"Why Mr. Lee, I'm sure I don't know what you mean."

"Mr. Faulkner, bandits, grave-robbers really, are using this town as their headquarters."

"Oh dear," the Reverend sighed. "Mr. Lee. Mr. Lee will you walk with me." The Reverend began to pace up and down on the stony soil, clearly searching for words. Finally he walked to the church, itself, and let them both in the back door with a key. "You know Reuben that the Lord forgives a sinner. Can we do less?"

"We don't need to wear the clothes the sinners steal for us," Reuben replied, "Or furnish our churches with their stolen property."

He gestured toward the desk at which Mr. Faulkner was sitting and at the big leather-bound Bible resting on the desktop.

The minister pursed his lips. "Have you talked to anyone else about this?" he asked.

"I've talked to Abe."

"Abe Simpson; yes, a good man. And Pegleg, you've talked to Pegleg."

"Yes, I did. Well, not really."

"Perhaps you should talk to him now," the minister said. He stood up from his chair.

The minister walked Reuben to the general store. Clearly, he wanted to rid himself of a disagreeable and difficult task. "Pegleg," the minister began, "Mr. Lee is not satisfied with many of the ways of our town."

"We can't keep taking these things," Reuben said before Pegleg could reply.

"We can't afford not to," said Pegleg. "Many of us lost all we had when we first came out here. Some to the Apache. Some to these same bandits. Our lives were all we had and we were grateful. Now we've got a town, a church, a minister. You've seen the farms; we're making a good living here. All of us are. I hurt my back or I'd be out tending my own farm. And confidentially," Pegleg leaned over the counter conspiratorially, "these bandits ain't gonna piss in their own washtub. So we don't got no problems that way." As the bell rang in the doorway behind them, Pegleg raised his voice, "And another satisfied customer."

Spring stood in the mercantile doorway, Helen beside her. Spring was carrying Helen's new dress still wrapped in the paper it had come in. "Wrong size? No problem," said Pegleg, "I told you there would be no problem with exchanges."

"We don't want to exchange it," Spring said, "We just wanted to bring it back."

"Bring it back! I see," said PegLeg, "Yours is a very holy group. What is it the bible says, Reverend, 'Let he who is without sin cast ...'"

"I didn't say we were without sin..." Reuben began.

"It's a very pretty dress, really," Helen said at the same time. Each of them stopped and waited for the other to continue.

The mercantile bell sounded a second time and Abe Simpson walked into the store.

"The Lee's are pretty upset," said Pegleg.

"Perhaps rightly so," corrected the Reverend. He fingered a pair of wool pants, absent-mindedly, thinking ahead to winter.

"I thought we talked about this," Abe said to Reuben ignoring the others.

"I'm not sure you were listening," Reuben replied.

"Damn fool," Abe said to no one in particular. He walked over to Pegleg and began an intense conversation of which Reuben could make out only a few phrases. The Reverend Faulkner launched a more light-hearted conversation with Helen who was soon laughing and talking animatedly.

"Does he know who's here?" Reuben heard Abe say. The meaning of this remark only made sense to Reuben later.

When Abe finished his discussion, he invited them back into the cantina. "Sit down and eat something. My treat," Abe said to Spring. "Your husband may be more easy to reason with on a full stomach."

She's not my wife, Reuben thought, but they had too much else to argue about.

The dark cavernous interior of the cantina contrasted sharply with the hot bright storefront. Temporarily blind, Reuben had no choice but to thread his way helplessly between the tables in Abe's wake.

"I don't think....," Reuben began.

"We won't talk until we have something in our stomachs," Abe said firmly. "Now what do you want to eat?"

"What have they got?" Reuben asked.

"Mainly Mexican, but Maria's a great cook, she can fix anything you like. You ladies are in for a treat. Do you like spicy?"

Helen and Spring looked at each other. "Spicy for me, not so spicy for Helen," Spring said.

"That's just the way my family is," said Abe. Now how about you Reuben?"

"Eggs," he said.

"Eggs it is. And with some of Maria's special ranch sauce," Abe said to the waiter, a young dark-haired Mexican boy whom Reuben could not remember having seen before.

"We'd like you people to stay," Abe said to them when the waiter had left. "Look. We like you people very much. I think there's a place for you here."

"But you must understand," Spring began, "we were captured by the Indians, Helen and I, used as slaves. I lost a husband. Helen lost a father."

"We've all lost husbands, wives. This is the West. But the thing is, you're safe here. Indians don't attack us. Bandits neither."

"Because you are the bandits," Reuben cried, but Abe ignored him:

"You three have been all over right? New Orleans, St Louis, Santa Fe. Have you ever seen a place like this out West before? All the water you could need. Crops springing out of the ground. Corn, melons, lettuce. Oh, and here's our food now. I tell you it will be delicious."

The women ate as if they had never seen food before, but as far as Reuben was concerned the food was tasteless, unappetizing. I would rather chew stale buffalo hide then be sitting here gossiping with this man, he thought.

Reuben's eyes had adjusted finally to the darkness. While the others concentrated on their food, he gazed about the large room. They could feed a hundred people at a time inside this building, Reuben thought. Tables were everywhere. Some were no more than long planks stretched over sawhorses. Others, like the one they sat at, were of fine iron lacework with marble tops. And all were probably stolen from some wagon train, its occupants first butchered, then robbed of even their clothes.

"What are you worried about?" said Abe. "Being captured and taken prisoner again? You're safe here." Spring and Helen had stopped chewing, their attention focused on Abe. "The Apache won't come here. We're too strong. Oh, they might come to trade, maybe. And the bandits won't come here either, because, well..."

"Because this is where the bandits live," Reuben said brutally.

Across from them in the dark corner next to the mercantile's doorway sat two tables of swarthy men. The bandit chief sat at one of them, still wearing his resplendent gold sash. It was the gold that glowed in the faint light of the doorway, that gleamed and glittered each time he moved.

Next to the bandit chief was his swarthy lieutenant, heavily muscled, with broad thick shoulders, his mouth scarred and twisted into a permanent sneer. One of the man's huge hands clutched a brown glass bottle by the neck, the other lay loosely palm upward on the table. Near it, inches from the thick fingers, a large hunting knife waited to be put to use.

Two other men sat at the bandit chief's table, their backs to Reuben. Between them and their chief were two empty chairs, legs tilted upward in the air.

The second table was filled with men, some eating, all taking huge gulps from the brown glass bottles, though it was still early in the morning. From time to time, a man would be called over from the second table to sit next to the bandit chief. One of the tilted chairs would be turned upright, the man would sit down, and the bandit chief would talk to him intently for some minutes.

Between visits, it seemed to Reuben the bandit chief was looking across at their table, staring intently at one and then the other of them. Reuben looked to see if the others had noticed. Spring was in intense conversation with Abe. But Helen sat frozen, her eyes riveted on the tall Mexican.

At that moment, the bandit chief reached across the table, drew his lieutenant's head over close to his own and whispered in his ear. The lieutenant nodded in the direction of Reuben's table. An instant later, he stood up and walked over toward them. His knife, Reuben saw, was no longer on the table.

"The Don wishes to buy the white woman," the man said in Spanish. He looked directly at Helen as he spoke. A flow of furious Spanish followed, first from Spring, then from the man.

"She's not for sale," said Reuben when the words had finally been translated for his benefit. Apparently, Spring had passed on the message only when forced to.

"The Don offers $200 in gold," said the man. "It is a fair price. He could just take your woman."

"What's happening?" said Helen, "What's going on?"

"Abe," said Reuben, but Abe was gone. He had disappeared from their table at almost the same moment the bandit had crossed over to them.

"Make up your mind, Señor," said the bandit. All pretense that he was talking through Spring had been abandoned.

The room had quieted. All eyes were focused on him and the bandit. For the first time, Reuben realized how noisy the room had been.

The young Mexican boy that had been their waiter stepped between the two men and carefully removed the empty plates from the table. Only Reuben's untouched eggs were left sitting before them. When the boy left, the knife appeared as if by magic in the lieutenant's hand.

Reuben's arm flicked out, his own knife in his extended hand. The bandit gave a small cry and dropped his weapon. Drops of bright red blood oozed slowly from his wrist where Reuben had nicked him.

A swish of drawn guns sounded from all around them, followed by a series of clicks as the guns were cocked. The bandits' guns were all pointed at their table. Reuben had only the one gun, his rifle, but it was pointed at the bandit chief.

For a long time, all of them held their positions, the bandits trying to stare him down. Then one of the bandits moved forward. Immediately, Reuben waved him back, gesturing with his rifle at the bandit chief's chest.

"Mexican standoff," Reuben said.

The bandit chief laughed. "You want to come with me, pretty Helen?" he called, speaking in English.

"No way," she said, but she did not move closer to Reuben.

"You stay with him, you be a farmer's wife, no better than an Indian. Your skin get all red and wrinkled from the sun, your hair turn gray. You come with me to California, you live in a ranchero, like a princess. You wear dresses brought from Madrid. You are the mother of one thousand acres and when the peasants, they see you walk by, they take off their hats like this."

"Helen..." Reuben began, but he did not know what else to say. He sat tight and hunched in his chair while the bandit chief made extravagant gestures with his hat and his free hand.

"You and I will give parties for the other great ranchers. You will have a hundred peasants to serve at the dinner and you will have ten times a hundred candles on the dining room table and lining the hallways. There will be brightness everywhere and dancing."

"And dancing," Helen echoed. Her face was flushed and excited as it had been the night of the barn dance. Then it darkened. "But you are a bandit," she said.

"No more;" the bandit chief replied, "the soldiers come. We take our gold and return to my ranch. And you come with me pretty Helen."

Reuben had taken out his six-gun and placed it first on the table and then in his other hand. Now the six-gun was pointed at the bandit chief while the rifle was free to roam up and down, up and down the row of bandits.

The bandits' guns were cocked and extended before them, but none rushed to be the first to fire.

"Come with me pretty Helen. Come," the bandit chief repeated.

"All right," she said, her voice sounding as if she were mesmerized; she began to walk slowly across the room toward the bandit chief. "Goodbye, Reuben," she said, but she did not look back as the bandit chief's arm wrapped about her shoulders and he led her from the room.

"Wait," Reuben said. But no one turned to look at him. The bandit chief seemed almost indifferent to Reuben's six-gun. The other bandits too seemed to have lost interest in them and had turned to leave.

Only the swarthy lieutenant remained behind. "I too would like a good woman," he said. His words were in Spanish but the meaning was clear. He stared at Spring's body, openly lustful; his eyes traveling slowly over her hips and her breasts. Her posture registered total disdain. He moved his eyes upward until they locked glances; when she looked away, his glance dropped to her bosom again and he smiled. The other bandits had stopped and were watching him. He reached for her.

Reuben shot him. The big man screamed and clapped his hand to his shoulder. Reuben could hear the click as a dozen guns were cocked and pointed toward him.

"No!" It was the bandit chief, calling his men off. "Felipe," he cooed to his lieutenant, "What are you doing?" The injured bandit replied with a torrent of guttural Spanish. "No, Felipe; come away. It is not necessary." He added an additional sentence in Spanish that Reuben did not catch. Reluctantly, teeth-barred, the injured man backed away from Reuben toward the front of the room.

The other bandits put away their guns, and for the second time, Reuben was left alone, six-gun in one outstretched hand, rifle in the other, squared off against an indifferent enemy.

Now, thought Reuben, he'll do it now. And as the injured bandit passed the table where he had been sitting with his chief, he whirled and threw his knife.

Reuben dropped to the floor. In the same movement, he flipped over the table to give Spring something to hide behind. He was shooting and leaping toward the back wall as the bandits were aiming and firing.

There was a brief flurry of gunshots, a scream of pain, and then a deathly quiet.

"You O.K., Spring?" he asked. He could sense her off to the side but he could not see her.

There was no reply. Where are you Spring? Periodically, he would fire toward the open doorway, but the bandits no longer seemed to be returning his fire. "Do you think they're gone?" he asked.

"No," came Spring's voice. She was alive then. "You shot him," she said, wonderingly, almost savoring each word.

"Who?"

"The pig." She made an expansive gesture with her hand, her face registering half a dozen conflicting emotions as she turned toward Reuben.

Reuben could hear a crackling like a series of muffled explosions somewhere in the distance. A red-yellow light flickered in the mercantile doorway. "I smell smoke," he said.

Chapter 20

"Get down on the floor," said Reuben and knelt on one knee to show Spring what he intended: "See, the smoke rises. If we stay close to the floor, we'll be able to get air a little longer."

The bandits had carefully piled the wooden tables at the front of the room, blocking the only exit, before setting them on fire. He could smell the kerosene they'd used to start the green wood burning. The fire had spread rapidly from the tables to the walls of the building and then to the mercantile at the front of the cantina.

A roof beam burnt free and fell across a tabletop releasing a shower of sparks. For a moment, it rested there glowing, and then both the roof beam and the table burst into flame. The harsh, acrid aroma tore at his lungs.

At first, he had been unable to find Spring. Blinded by the gunshots, he'd groped behind the table where he'd thought she was hiding, then crawled painfully along the floor toward the rear of the cantina until he heard her, calling, only a few feet from where he'd left her.

She knelt on all fours like some kind of animal, her head raised toward the ceiling. "Get down," he said unnecessarily.

Spring had remained huddled behind the table, shivering with fright, until suddenly, she became conscious Reuben was no longer at her side. Then she had run after him in the darkness, only to bruise her thighs and shins on one of the remaining tables and collapse to her knees.

The crackling at the front of the cantina had become a roar. Smoke was gusting back and forth across the middle of the room, lit from within like some poet's version of hell. It became increasingly more difficult to breathe; Reuben and Spring were forced to move farther and farther away from the exit toward the far wall to avoid the flames.

A wall of fire swept across the room in front of them and they could hear the collapsing timbers. If they stayed where they were, they would die; if they left, the bandits would shoot them.

They had to get out of the room and soon before the ceiling collapsed. But the café had only the one door, straight ahead, through the smoke and the flames.

"Put your kerchief over your nose and mouth and follow me," Reuben said. He started to crawl toward the front of the building. "No," she said, "they'll be waiting outside for you to do that. They'll want you to stay and dance in the flames. It's safer here."

"Safer?" he questioned.

"The walls of the cantina are made of clay, adobe. The front of the building where they added on the mercantile is all wood. See, the front is the only part of the cantina that is burning."

"And the tables." He began to push and shove the tables near them toward the front of the room, clearing a space, but broke into a fit of coughing.

"Get down," she said, and pulled him down beside her to lie on the cold floor. "Hold on to my waist. We'll crawl to the back of the room and wait there till the flames die down."

"How will we breathe?" he asked.

"The same way we are now; we've got to be getting air from someplace."

They sat on the floor against the back wall, watching as the flames progressed across the room jumping from table to table. "The wall is solid adobe," he said. "We're trapped. As soon as we run out of air, we die."

"No, there has to be a crack in the wall," Spring insisted, "there has to be. I'm going to look for it."

"Stay near me," he called, begging, and crawled after her.

The room had almost filled with smoke, except for a thin wedge of clear air next to the floor, when Spring announced, "I've found it. A crack; not a large one, but we'll have fresh air. Crawl along next to me until you come to it."

He slid his body along the floor keeping his body between her and the flames. He could feel her breasts pressing against him from behind. "I can't find the opening," he said.

Grasping his fingers as if he were a blind man, she guided his hand forward until it came in contact with a narrow crack in the adobe wall. Then, he had his face jammed up against it and was taking deep gasping breaths. "Thanks," he said.

The crack started at floor level and went up no more than two feet before it closed together. In that brief length, the opening was wide enough that the two lying side by side on the floor could not only press against it for air but also could get a brief uncluttered look at the street outside.

Nothing moved in the empty street, though they could hear the sound of horses and shots being fired into the air at the front of the building. They lay for a while side by side next to the opening; he continued to be conscious of and embarrassed by her bosoms pressing into him from behind.

"Maybe we should try to get out, find something to widen the hole with?" he said.

"Not yet. We want them to think we're dead. Wait till it's dark. Wait till they've all gone."

He was conscious of her strong arms holding him. Of her perfumed hair on his cheek, and then of the kisses she was raining

onto his own hair and on his cheeks. "I love you Spring," he said
and he turned so that his lips met her lips and they lay quietly
together kissing for a long time.

She removed her skirt and placed the double folds under her on
the floor. He fumbled with his own belt until finally she had to help
him with that. "I'm thirty-two," he said.

Chapter 21

When they woke, it was very late, almost dusk. The guns were silent, though they could still hear the sounds of voices murmuring in the distance. Even as he broke a hole in the adobe with the butt of his rifle, Reuben was conscious that behind them where the wooden store and cantina had once stood was only charred embers and that the murmuring on the other side of the burned-out building was a funeral procession.

"Our horses are gone," he said, almost his first comment after sliding out into the street. Spring gave him a long penetrating look and waited for him to complete his thought. "I was hoping they would be," Reuben said defensively, "I mean I was hoping that Champion and the others would have a chance to get away and all. I would not have liked them to be hurt in the fire."

Our horses are halfway to Mexico now with the bandits, Spring thought but said nothing. They were alive, she and Reuben, that notion in itself was so wonderful that nothing else could spoil it.

I love you Reuben, she thought.

When they had circled the building, they found the townspeople at the front of the store sifting through the embers. "All gone," said the Reverend still clutching the bible. A bucket of water would have been a mite more useful, Spring Morning thought but held her tongue. "I was praying for you son," the Reverend said, "praying for you both."

"We could have used an extra gun," said Reuben.

"Too many of them," said Pegleg apologetically. He had reappeared magically along with Abe and several of the other townspeople who had been in the cafe when the trouble started.

"You're out of a job, Pegleg. You've got nothing to put on your shelves," Spring chuckled and Reuben laughed aloud. "He can always farm," Reuben said, "'less'n he's afraid of hard work."

"You two going to stay around town?" the storekeeper asked as if he'd not heard what they said or, worse, had heard and chosen not to understand.

"Maybe," said Reuben.

"We can always use good people," the storekeeper continued. Reuben looked at him puzzled. Hadn't he heard what Spring said? Couldn't he see for himself what had happened? His store would never open again. This town would never again be able to live off the efforts of others. And then Reuben realized what Pegleg was really saying: With the bandits gone, they would need one another; the townspeople would need Reuben to protect them from Indians and bandits, just as Reuben and Spring would need them for supplies and company.

"The bandits won't be back," said Spring.

"Won't be back?" echoed Mrs. Crockett, her voice uncertain.

"They heard the soldiers were coming. They knew it was all over for them once the soldiers were here."

But Mrs., Crockett was not listening. "I'll miss that calico dress you had on display Mr. Pegleg. It was such a pretty dress."

"Praise the Lord," said the Reverend.

Reuben and Spring walked out of town toward their campsite, toward where the three from the big canyon had lived as a family, Reuben and Spring and Helen.

Their horses were gone. The free clothing, and the seed and farm tools on easy credit were history. All they had were their bedrolls and the contents of their saddlebags.

One last ray of sunlight streaked across the valley and reflected from the canyon wall, turning the land around them to pink and orange and red.

"It's good farmland here," Reuben said. "And I'm a good farmer. All the Lee's are."

"You're going to stay here?" Spring asked tentatively. "Not go to California?"

"I'm going to stay here and farm. Do you want to stay here Spring?

"Where I come from ...," Reuben began and then stopped.

"Yes, she said, "Go on." For a moment she felt a tinge of fear. Reuben had taken his arm from around her waist, the arm that had been there almost continuously since they'd walked together from the burned-out building. Was he planning to leave her?

"Where I come from, they hate niggers. They hate Indians, too. And Mexicans," he added before she could speak a second time. "They hate the French and they hate the Spanish. They hate Catholics and they hate Jews. They're a hating people. Come to think of it, they never liked me very much. So I ain't going back to Louisiana. And I ain't going to St Louis, now. Or California.

"You want to stay here with me Spring and raise cotton and babies?"

Cotton and babies, he'd said to her. She guessed this was as close as he would get to a marriage proposal. "Boys and girls," she said smiling, "little Reuben, little Spring Morning."

"Just boys," he said. "Come to think of it, I don't like little girls very much." They both laughed. He put his arm around her and this time he did not take it away.

Did you like this novel? You might also want to read a second exciting western by author Luke Jackson, *The Gunfighter*.

In 1874, when David Marsall arrived in the Wyoming Territory by train from Philadelphia, tired, hungry and virtually penniless, he had no idea that in a few short weeks he would be called "The Gunfighter."

In his own mind, David was a failure. While his brother lay a hero on the field at Gettysburg, David had spent the war years adding endless columns of figures. The small amount he embezzled barely bought him a coach class ticket to Morgan City WY. And in Morgan City, David found clean white shirts and high starched collars were no substitute for calloused hands and a pair of sturdy work boots.

Ollie Swenson gave him a job, grudgingly. But then Ollie had begrudged everyone and everything since his wife died.

Selling otherwise worthless land to Ollie and his group of Swedish immigrants had seemed a good idea to Pontius Morgan at the time, but now their fences were ruining "his" grazing land. He offered to buy them out—for ten cents on the dollar—and when they wouldn't sell, he turned to other methods of persuasion.

David came out from hiding to drive off Morgan's hired killers. The news gave the other settlers backbone. And it made Morgan angry enough to send East for another dozen thugs.

Other characters in this exciting book include ten-year old Arnold Jensen who portrays Mr. Lincoln in the school play, the widow Danielle Lemieux—she liked David; so what if he were ten years younger—and Jake Flemming, a hell of a nice guy—he'd buy you a beer even if it was his job to gun you down.

Purchase and read your copy of *The Gunfighter* today. Go to http://zanybooks.com.